TIME CAT

OTHER YEARLING BOOKS YOU WILL ENJOY:

YEARLING BOOKS/YOUNG YEARLINGS/YEARLING CLASSICS are designed especially to entertain and enlighten young people. Patricia Reilly Giff, consultant to this series, received her bachelor's degree from Marymount College and a master's degree in history from St. John's University. She holds a Professional Diploma in Reading and a Doctorate of Humane Letters from Hofstra University. She was a teacher and reading consultant for many years, and is the author of numerous books for young readers.

For a complete listing of all Yearling titles, write to
Dell Readers Service,
P.O. Box 1045,
South Holland, IL 60473.

TIME CAT

Lloyd Alexander

Illustrated by Bill Sokol

A YEARLING BOOK

Published by
Dell Publishing
a division of
Bantam Doubleday Dell Publishing Group, Inc.
666 Fifth Avenue
New York, New York 10103

ISBN: 0-440-48677-7

Reprinted by arrangement with Holt, Rinehart and Winston

Printed in the United States of America

First Yearling printing—September 1985

10 9 8 7 6 5 4

CWO

Contents

1.
The Visitors

Gareth was a black cat with orange eyes. Sometimes, when he hunched his shoulders and put down his ears, he looked like an owl. When he stretched, he looked like a trickle of oil or a pair of black silk pajamas. When he sat on a window ledge, his eyes half-shut and his tail curled around him, he looked like a secret.

He belonged to a boy named Jason, who loved him and believed Gareth could do anything in the world. As things turned out, Jason was right—not entirely, but almost.

It happened this way.

In the middle of a sunny afternoon, Jason sat in his room on the end of his bed, with his chin in his hands, and wished the past five minutes had never happened.

Downstairs, in that space of time, he had accomplished the following:

1/ Spilled paint on the dining-room table.
2/ Dropped his model airplane and stepped on it.
3/ Coated the inside of one pocket of his jacket with

glue, when the tube he had been saving for emergencies had come uncapped.

4/ Torn his shirt.

5/ Punched his younger brother in the ribs for laughing at him.

6/ Talked back to his mother, who had not agreed his brother needed punching.

7/ Begun to cry, a thing Jason despised because he considered himself too old for it.

There had been other details he preferred to forget. In any case, he had been told to go to his room, which he did, feeling put down and miserably sorry for himself.

Gareth, who had been drowsing on top of Jason's pillow, uncurled and climbed onto the boy's lap. Jason stroked the cat and ran his finger over Gareth's only white spot—on his chest, a T-shaped mark with a loop over the crossbar.

"Lucky Gareth," Jason sighed, lying back and closing his eyes, "I wish *I* had nine lives."

The cat stopped purring. "I wish I did, too," he said.

Jason started up in surprise. Not because Gareth had spoken. Jason had always been sure he could if he wanted to. It was what Gareth had said.

"You mean you really don't have nine lives?" Jason asked, disappointed.

"I'm afraid not," said the cat, in a very matter-of-fact way. "But, since you mention it, I'll tell you a secret. I only have one life. With a difference: I can visit."

"Visit?" Jason said.

"Yes," Gareth went on, "I can visit nine different lives. Anywhere, any time, any country, any century."

"Oh, Gareth!" Jason clapped his hands. "Can all cats do that?"

"Where do you think cats go when you're looking all over and can't find them?" Gareth replied. "And have you ever noticed a cat suddenly appear in a room when you were sure the room was empty? Or disappear, and you can't imagine where he went?"

"And you've actually gone to a lot of different countries?" Jason asked.

"No, not yet," Gareth said. "I've been waiting for—oh, I don't know, a special occasion, you might say. I never saw much sense in just going as a tourist. It's better to wait until there's some important reason."

"I guess you're right," Jason nodded. He looked over at Gareth. "I was wondering if you thought there might be a special occasion coming up soon?"

"There might be," said Gareth.

"Gareth, listen," Jason said eagerly, "if it were a special occasion and somebody else, somebody you liked, wanted very much to go, could you take him with you?"

Gareth did not answer immediately. He began looking like an owl and stayed that way for a while. Finally, he said, "Yes, I suppose I could."

"Would you take me?"

Gareth was silent again. "I could take you with me," he said, after a moment, "but I have to warn you of this. You'd be on your own, you wouldn't have any kind of protection. Neither of us would. Naturally, I'd help you every way I could; we'd be able to talk to each other, but only when no one else was around. Aside from that, what happens, happens. And you couldn't change your mind in the middle.

"Oh, there's something else. Whatever you did, you wouldn't dare be separated from me for any length of time. Otherwise, you'd never see home again. Now, if you accept the conditions . . ."

"Oh, Gareth, I accept!"

"Are you sure?" the cat asked. "Think carefully."

Jason nodded.

"Very well," said the cat. "Look into my eyes." And he gave Jason a long, slow wink.

Egypt

·

2700 B.C.

2.
The Sacred City
of Cats

A white sun, a green-blue sky. In a grove of palm trees, a temple rose at the end of a long avenue. Jason, with Gareth at his side, walked through a courtyard that seemed to stretch for miles.

"Why . . . we're in Egypt," Jason said in a hushed voice.

He knew this with certainty, then wondered how he knew. He suspected that Gareth had somehow given him the knowledge.

Jason saw that even his clothing was Egyptian—a length of white linen tied about his waist. Perhaps this was all a part of the cat's strange powers. "We've really come this far!"

"We could have gone farther," Gareth said, "but this is a good place to start. For a cat, at least. The Egyptians worship us, you know."

"Worship cats?"

"Indeed they do," Gareth said. "They're fond of us— just as cats, you understand. And they worship us, too. They have all kinds of sacred animals, but the cat—ah, the cat is most important. We're sacred to the great goddess Ubaste of the Sun and Moon."

In the distance, Jason heard the sound of flutes and drums approaching. Gareth stopped in front of a statue of Ubaste herself. Cat-headed, she wore a long, clinging robe; in one hand, the goddess held a sacred rattle; in the other, a shield. At her feet crouched four stone kittens.

Gareth leaped to the base of the statue. "There's a festival every year, here in Bubastis," he said. "It's the sacred city of the cat goddess, and the ceremonies are very fancy. Get behind the statue and you can watch. I'll stay here."

Gareth squeezed himself in among the kittens. With his tail curled around in front of him, his ears up, he sat as motionless as the statue itself.

The music grew louder. Worshipers began to fill the courtyard. Jason couldn't begin to count them, but he guessed there must be thousands.

Lines of white-robed priests swayed along the avenue toward the temple. Some carried sacred rattles; others held staves topped by glittering, golden statues of cats. Chanting voices filled the air with the "Hymn to the Great Cat":

Thy head is the head of the Sun-God,
Thy nose is the nose of Thoth;
Thine ears are the ears of Osiris
Who hears the voice of all who call upon him.

Jason understood the language as if he had always known it. Was this more of Gareth's magic?

The music of the flutes wavered like pale blue streaks against the clouds. As the procession passed, the crowd followed after. Some were dressed in robes or skirts of linen. They carried great baskets of flowers and trays of fruit.

The worshipers took up the chant:

Thy mouth is the mouth of Atum
Thy heart is the heart of Ptah;
Thy teeth are the teeth of the Moon-God.

The music and singing filled Jason's whole body as the hymn continued:

Thy whiskers are the rays of the Sun;
Thine eyes hold the Sun and Moon.

Then it stopped, and there was silence, as if the top of the sky had been lifted off. All at once, a powerful voice cried out:

"Hear us, Great Cat, Sayer of Great Words!"

The temple doors were opening. The worshipers streamed up the white steps. Finally, when the last of the crowd had passed, Jason ventured out from behind the statue, hoping to follow them.

He had taken no more than two steps when something gripped him tightly and uncomfortably. Jason twisted around and found himself looking up at a white-robed, shaven-headed man who scowled angrily at him. With one hand, the man held a roll of papyrus; with the other, Jason's ear.

"Wretched boy," cried the man, "reveal your business here! If you come to worship at the temple, why do you hide behind the statue?"

There were several scribes, Jason saw, all carrying bundles of papyrus scrolls or clay tablets. Just then Gareth hopped down, and as soon as the Chief Scribe caught sight of him, he let go of Jason's ear.

"Behold! Behold this cat! On his chest he bears the mark of the sacred ankh, symbol of life!"

The scribes dropped to their knees. Gareth sat down and began to wash.

After the scribes had got through worshiping, and Gareth had got through washing, the Chief Scribe reached into a fold of his robe and brought out a leather purse.

"My dear friend," said the Chief Scribe in an oily voice, "forgive me for pinching your ear. I didn't realize you were accompanied by such a distinguished and curiously marked creature. Tell me one thing. How much gold will you take for him?"

"Sell my cat?" Jason cried indignantly.

"O crafty maker of letters," interrupted one of the Minor Scribes, "it would be less expensive if we simply took this cat and left the boy in care of the sacred crocodiles."

The Chief Scribe stroked his chin and looked carefully at Jason. "Your suggestion has merit," he said. "I was, in fact, about to say the same thing."

"O learned keeper of the scrolls," a Sub-minor Scribe timidly ventured, "remember the cat bears the sacred ankh. It is a powerful sign. Who knows what vengeance he might take?"

"My objection exactly," said the Chief Scribe.

"I don't know who you are," Jason burst in, "but I don't think you have any right to stand there and talk about taking somebody's cat away—and throwing somebody else to the crocodiles."

"I'm afraid," said the Chief Scribe, "that you don't understand. For many months we have sought the one cat in all Egypt that will be able to please the mighty ruler of the Great House, King Neter-Khet—may he have life, health, and strength!"

"Life! Health! Strength!" shouted the Minor Scribes. "Life! Health! Strength!" echoed the Sub-minor Scribes.

"And so," went on the Chief Scribe, "when we saw your cat, and the mark on his chest, it occurred to us that he might indeed be the one. Under those circumstances, my young friend, we entreat you to come to the Great House and allow the Lord of the Two Lands of Egypt to gaze upon your cat."

"Well . . ." Jason said reluctantly, "I suppose he could gaze if he wanted to. But that's all."

"Naturally," said the Chief Scribe, smiling blandly. "No one would dream of forcing you to do anything against your will."

"All right, then," Jason said. "But don't forget. Only gazing."

"Your head is full of wisdom," said the Chief Scribe. "I can tell you now: if you hadn't agreed, you'd have very likely had to take your chances with the crocodiles."

"Yes," Jason sighed, "that's what I thought."

The scribes led Jason and Gareth to the river and down a flight of stone steps where the royal barge waited. Once all had climbed aboard, the oarsmen shoved off and began rowing at top speed.

For several days the barge skimmed along the Nile. Finally, Jason asked how long it would be until they reached the Great House.

"Unenlightened boy," said the Chief Scribe, "we have been traveling through it since yesterday."

At last, the oarsmen docked at the riverbank. The Great House, Jason realized, was a whole city in itself, with bakers, carpenters, brickmakers, weavers. Holding Gareth tightly, Jason followed the Chief Scribe to the biggest building of all. They stopped in one hall filled with nothing but men marking on clay tablets. Here, messengers never ceased hurrying in and shouting commands from King Neter-Khet.

In the space of a few minutes, from what Jason could hear, Neter-Khet had declared five wars, signed three peace treaties, and ordered eight thousand stonemasons to begin a new pyramid. There was also a constant procession of slaves dragging in goods of all kinds. The scribes made a great ceremony of scratching down their tallies. The Egyptians, Jason decided, loved to count things. Nobody, as far as he saw, could do anything without mentioning quantities, writing them down, comparing, adding, and marveling at the totals.

The Chief Scribe approached one of the clerks. "In the records of the Great House make this notation: this day, to the possessions of Pharaoh—life, health, strength—there shall be added forty thousand bushels of grain, seventy thousand jars of oil, three thousand ounces of gold, and one black cat."

"So it was spoken," said the clerk, "so it is written!"

"Oh no it won't!" Jason cried. "My cat isn't one of Pharaoh's possessions!"

"It would seem," said the Chief Scribe, with a cold smile, "that he is now."

Before Jason could turn and race from the hall, the Chief Scribe scooped the bristling, spitting Gareth from his arms. Jason himself was seized from behind, hustled down a corridor, and most unceremoniously shoved into a tiny room.

3.
Neter-Khet

The heavy stone door swung shut behind him. Jason beat at it with his fists. He had never trusted the oily words of the Chief Scribe. How, Jason thought furiously, had he let himself be tricked so easily? He threw himself against the unyielding door; then, exhausted, dropped to the ground. Now Gareth was gone. Jason would spend the rest of his life in a stone cell in Neter-Khet's palace. The boy hid his face in his hands and his shoulders shook with sobbing. At least, he consoled himself, the Egyptians loved cats and Gareth would be well looked after.

To Jason's surprise, a little while later the door opened and a Sub-minor Scribe peered in. Jason scrambled to his feet. Behind the Sub-minor Scribe were two guards, who took him by the arms and marched him from the cell down one hall of columns after the other, until Jason lost track of them all. In a huge room at the end of one corridor, on a platform topped by a carved and decorated throne, sat King Neter-Khet.

Beside the King stood slaves with fly whisks and feathered fans on jeweled poles, musicians with trumpets and cymbals, and the Chief Scribe himself, looking sour. In front of the throne sat Gareth. The cat, Jason saw, was watching Neter-Khet in much the same way that he would watch a beetle or something else that interested him—but didn't interest him very much.

"Great King, live forever," said the Chief Scribe. "This is the wretch we found lurking behind the statue. Perhaps his presence here will help."

"We shall see," said Neter-Khet.

In his high headdress and robes, arms crossed in front of him and holding the shepherd's crook and flail of divine authority, the Pharaoh looked no different from the statues in the throne room. But Neter-Khet's face was dark and frowning. He looked, Jason thought, as if he never stopped being angry.

"I COMMAND THIS CAT TO PLAY AND ENTERTAIN PHARAOH!" shouted King Neter-Khet at the top of his voice.

The musicians clashed their cymbals. The slaves cried "Life! Health! Strength!" and the fly-whisker whisked as fast as he could.

Gareth did not move.

"Well, go ahead, boy!" hissed the Chief Scribe. "Make the cat be entertaining!"

Jason hesitated, then knelt on the floor beside Gareth. One of the slaves tossed down a toy, a bejeweled mouse on a golden chain. Jason pulled it back and forth in front of the cat, but he could tell from the set of Gareth's ears and whiskers that he was in no mood for games.

Jason dropped the toy and shook his head. "He doesn't want to," he said. "I'm afraid there isn't anything I can do."

Neter-Khet looked angrier than ever.

"I COMMAND THIS CAT TO PURR AND MAKE HIMSELF AGREEABLE TO PHARAOH!" he shouted.

Once again there was a clashing of cymbals and cries of "Life! Health! Strength!"

The Chief Scribe took out a clay tablet. "So it is ordered," he said, "so it is written, and so it shall be done!"

Gareth still did not move. Jason shrugged hopelessly, then picked up Gareth and put him on Neter-Khet's lap. The King began stroking him, but Gareth put down his ears and squinted his eyes. He wriggled out of Pharaoh's arms and leaped to the floor.

"Aiee!" Neter-Khet put his thumb to his mouth. One of Gareth's claws had accidentally scratched the King, and Pharaoh's braided beard shook with rage.

"I'm sorry," Jason said. "He doesn't feel like playing or being agreeable right now. It's nothing personal," he added quickly, "it's the way cats are."

"It's obvious," said the Chief Scribe, "the boy is useless."

"Return the cat to Bubastis," ordered Neter-Khet. "He does not please me. Continue your search."

"And the boy?" asked the Scribe. "The sacred crocodiles are always hungry," he suggested cheerfully.

Neter-Khet closed his eyes and nodded.

"So it is ordered," said the Chief Scribe, making another note on his tablet, "so it shall be done." He gestured to the guards.

Once again Jason was seized and hustled down the vast corridors. He clung to Gareth and pressed his cheek against the cat's glossy fur. "I don't care what they do to me," Jason whispered, frightened though he was. "I'm glad you didn't entertain Pharaoh just because he ordered it. You be the way you are. That's all that counts. Don't worry," Jason added, "the sacred crocodiles probably won't be hungry anyway."

Jason heard a shout behind him. The guards stopped. It was Neter-Khet himself, waving his crook and flail. "Return the cat! Return the boy to me!"

As Jason and Gareth entered the throne room, the cymbals clashed again, the trumpets blew, and the slaves began plying their fans. "Stop that ridiculous whisking," Neter-Khet commanded. "Get out. All of you. You too," he said, pointing his flail at the Chief Scribe.

In the empty hall Neter-Khet seemed too tired to climb the steps to his throne. Instead, he slumped down on the edge of the platform. He took off his headdress, his wig, and, to Jason's amazement, even his braided beard. Without them Neter-Khet didn't appear half as angry as before.

"For the last time," he said, "are you sure there's nothing you can do? It's happened with every cat they've brought in. All my subjects worship me—I'm a god, you know—my slaves are building the finest pyramid in Egypt, so things will be comfortable for me in the Other World. But I can't find a cat to sit on my lap. And, after all, we're both sacred. It's beyond me. Absolutely beyond me."

Neter-Khet looked so discouraged and unhappy that Jason could not help feeling sorry for him.

"You can't imagine how I've longed for a cat of my own," Neter-Khet continued wistfully. "To stroke him and watch him play. When I was a child, I always had cats. They seemed very fond of me. Then, after I became Pharaoh, they didn't seem to care for me half as much."

Jason thought for a while. "I don't know," he said at last. "Did you wear that headdress and that beard before you got to be king? That might have frightened them. And another thing," he added, "did you shout as much? Cats don't like being shouted at."

Neter-Khet brightened a little. "That might be it."

"Even so," Jason said, "when you weren't shouting, you'd think they'd have come around again."

"Oh, they did," said Neter-Khet. "But they'd never play or purr when I ordered."

"Did you expect them to?" Jason said. "No cat in the world will do that!"

"But I'm Pharaoh," Neter-Khet said. "I'm supposed to give orders."

"That doesn't mean anything to a cat," said Jason. "Didn't anybody ever tell you?"

"Nobody tells *me*," Neter-Khet said. "I tell *them*. Besides, they were *my* cats, weren't they?"

"In a way they were," Jason said, "and in a way they weren't. A cat can *belong* to you, but you can't *own* him. There's a difference."

Gareth, meantime, had padded over to the disconsolate Pharaoh and now began to rub his head affectionately against Neter-Khet's ankles.

"LISTEN!" the King shouted, then clapped a hand to his mouth. "I mean, listen! He's purring," he whispered delightedly.

"But that's what I told you," Jason said. "All cats are friendly if you give them a chance. Once in a while they like to keep to themselves. They'll play and purr when *they* want to, and sometimes you have to wait. If you can understand that, I don't think you'll have any trouble at all finding a cat to please you. They'll please you by just being themselves."

Gareth had hopped on to the vacant throne and sat there watching them. Considering how touchy Neter-Khet was about being Pharaoh, Jason rose and started to pick up Gareth.

"No, let him stay there if he wants to," said Neter-Khet. "I have learned something this day. Not even Pharaoh can give orders to a cat."

Later, Neter-Khet summoned the Chief Scribe. "In the royal archives," said the King, "you have listed this cat as one of my possessions. That must be changed. Neither he nor any cat who shall live in the Great House shall be called a possession. Pharaoh is not his master, but his host and privileged friend."

"So it shall be written," said the Chief Scribe.

Neter-Khet turned to Jason. "I would be honored if you and your cat would choose to stay with me."

"We'd like to," said Jason, "but we have a long way to go."

Neter-Khet nodded. "So it shall be."

From his neck he took a golden ankh and hung it around Jason's own neck.

"Go in peace, strange travelers," he said. "You have made me wonder whether Ubaste herself did not send you."

Outside the Great House, Jason and Gareth followed a path along the river. "Well," Jason said, "I'm glad Neter-Khet found out that it doesn't do much good to shout a lot of orders."

"Certainly not at cats," Gareth said. "Or people, for that matter."

The air trembled in the sunset. Although far from Bubastis, it seemed to Jason he could still hear the strains of the "Hymn to the Great Cat."

"You know, Gareth," he said, "your whiskers do look like the rays of the sun. And I do think you could hold the moon in your eyes if you wanted to."

"So the Egyptians say," Gareth answered.

"Oh, Gareth," Jason whispered, "why don't you try?"

"Not right now," said Gareth. He winked.

And Egypt vanished.

Rome and Britain

•

55 B.C.

4.
The Old Cats Company

The wide avenues of Bubastis narrowed to a crowded street in Rome. Holding Gareth closely, Jason glanced around, wondering which way to turn. Before he could move, a hand fell on his shoulder.

"Here's the cat we want!"

Two soldiers, in close-fitting helmets and belted tunics, stepped up beside Jason. Stubby, businesslike swords hung at their waists. A shiny scar was scribbled across one man's forehead.

"Hold on there, we won't eat you," said the scarred man with a grin. "The Old Cats have velvet paws in Rome."

"And claws in Gaul," the second one laughed. He was shorter than his companion, but just as tough and leathery.

"Now then," said the first, "let's hear your report."

The soldier stiffened, and flung up his arm in a salute. "Marcus Arrius Bassus reports to Gaius Petronius Valens, centurion of the Old Cats Company. Mission: locate one cat for the honor of the Company. Mission accomplished!"

"What do you say to that?" the man called Petronius

asked Jason. "Not every cat gets a chance to join Caesar's legions. We need a mascot," he added, "and on the double. The Company's ordered back to Gaul."

"Always had a cat," Arrius put in. "For good luck, you know. There's a cat emblem on our standard, that's how we got our name."

"We still need a live one," said Petronius. "The Old Cats Company without a cat? We'd be ashamed to show our faces on parade."

"Our last cat ran off with a lop-eared tom," Arrius explained. "I said it was bound to happen," he added critically.

"So," Petronius said, disregarding Arrius' remark, "hand over the cat and we're off to Gaul."

He reached out.

Gareth hissed and wrinkled his lips.

"Oho," cried the centurion, "is that the way of it? Shows his teeth, eh? He's a legion cat, right enough."

Jason pulled himself up as tall as he could and looked the soldier in the eye, although the sword in Petronius' belt made Jason's voice shake a little. "This cat belongs with me."

"Bravely spoken!" Petronius clapped him on the shoulder. "And fair enough! We'll take both of you, then. Come on, there's nothing in Rome for a boy, and Rome's no place for a cat. Civilians don't appreciate cats. Put them in artichoke gardens to keep away moles, that's all *they* know. But the legions—fresh air, open sky, a good fight now and again. There's the life for a cat!"

"Any boy in Rome would give his ears to serve under Julius Caesar," Arrius said.

"See us on parade," Petronius went on. "The silver eagles in the sun, spears like a forest. And Caesar at the head of the column." At the word "Caesar," the face of Petronius shone with admiration and the leathery look softened.

"I don't know . . . ," Jason hesitated. The centurion's words trumpeted inside him, but he remembered what had happened in Egypt.

"When in doubt," Arrius said, "ask for an omen. That's army regulations."

"An omen," Petronius nodded. "In the legion we usually consult the sacred pigeons. I'm not going to chase after pigeons here; anyhow, that's a job for an expert. Well . . . I'll try something. Let's have that shield, Arrius."

Arrius unslung his shield and handed it over. Petronius, throwing his cloak aside, dropped to one knee.

"O Mars, god of battles, mighty Jupiter, father of the gods," he began, "or whatever it is the regimental augur says. Shall this boy and this cat march with us?" He gripped the shield and held it out flat in front of him. "Give us a sign."

Gareth, who had been watching the centurion with interest, leaped from Jason's arms and landed in the center of the shield. Arrius cheered and tossed his helmet in the air. The centurion raised the shield high in triumph. Gareth stood balanced on it, his tail like a banner, and with a special curl to his whiskers that, Jason knew, meant he was feeling exceptionally pleased.

"How's that for an omen?" asked Petronius. "The cat answers for himself!"

"You'll be proud you followed Caesar's eagles," Arrius said. "That's honor, courage . . ."

"Not artichokes!" added Petronius. "Come on, boy, we can't keep Caesar waiting. The Old Cats move fast!"

During the journey from Rome to Gaul, Jason couldn't decide which was worse: the tossing ship, powered by sails and oarsmen, or the cold marches through the forests once they had landed.

Gareth had no difficulties at all. He carried his tail as straight as a legionary's spear. With his lean, brisk walk and the determined arch of his neck, he seemed, to Jason, quite Roman. "I enjoy a comfortable bed," Gareth said, "but if there isn't one around, it doesn't matter. Any bed is soft to a cat."

Jason himself soon got used to camp life. By the time the Old Cats reached the western coast of Gaul, he could stride along with the best of them.

The Company joined the rest of Caesar's legions in a great encampment. From there, Caesar would lead the army across a narrow stretch of water to Britannica, a land even wilder than Gaul.

"But until he gives the orders," Petronius explained, "we've got a lot of work to do."

From dawn to sunset, Petronius and the other centurions drilled the legionaries in forming up in squares, throwing javelins, running, jumping, thrusting swords at stakes planted in the ground.

Too young for military duties—outside of cleaning breastplates and looking after the Company's baggage—Jason, with Gareth at his side, sat on the far edge of the flat clay field. Petronius' shouts of command carried through the chilly air. Gareth watched the drill with interest.

"These Romans know their business," said the cat. "It's worth seeing. Practice," he added. "That's what makes the difference. If you really want to be a professional, you've got to stick to it. We practice all the time." Gareth stood up and rippled his muscles. He made Jason think of somebody rolling up his sleeves before getting down to work. "Unless you knew," Gareth went on, "you might think we're only playing." He flicked his tail emphatically. "We aren't. Being a cat is a serious thing. Watch." Gareth lunged forward, pouncing hard, seizing a blade of grass with both front paws.

"I've seen you do that when you're playing with a cat-nip mouse," Jason called.

"Practicing for a real one," Gareth corrected. "It's the easiest kind of catch for anything on the ground. Here's a different one."

Balanced on three legs, Gareth curved one forepaw; faster than Jason's eye could follow, the cat scooped at the earth, and several mud clods bounced up in the air. "That's for something in the water," Gareth explained. "You have to move fast, and keep on scooping till you fish it out."

Without warning, Gareth leaped straight up, his front paws stretched above his head. As he leaped, he spun around and landed facing Jason. "That's for anything in the air," said the cat. "Those are the three simplest catches. But there's so much more: hunting positions, stalking positions, fighting positions."

"I didn't know it was so hard to be a cat," Jason said.

"Practice, practice," Gareth said. "Remember that."

The Romans had finished their drill. Shoulder pieces flashing, his face streaked with sweat and grime, Petronius sauntered over to the edge of the clay field. He waved his sword in greeting.

"Ho, there!" he called. "What are you doing, playing with your cat?"

Jason nodded, and smiled to himself.

That night it seemed Jason had barely gone to sleep before Petronius was shaking him to get up. The centurion's face was tense, the scar on his forehead shone in the torchlight, painfully white and new-looking.

"We're going over now," he said, in a hushed voice. "Here, put this on." He draped a cloak over Jason's shoulders. For a moment, the soldier held the boy close to him. Then Petronius suddenly turned brusque and warlike, shouting at the legionaries.

Jason wrapped part of the cloak around Gareth as a carrying sling.

Jason had no time to be frightened. Within moments the Old Cats formed up in ranks, with shields and swords ready, gripping their light throwing spears. Petronius gave a command and, with the rest of the legion, the Company moved toward the boats on the shore.

It was full morning, sunless and cold, when Jason first made out Britannica's chalky cliffs, jagged with the figures of men. As they came closer, Jason saw they held spears; it was then that he began feeling chilly, and even Gareth's fur against his side did not warm him. The Old Cats crouched silently in the rocking boat. Every man's face turned toward the cliffs. Petronius picked his way to where Jason sat huddled in his cloak. He gave the boy a wink and rubbed Gareth's chin.

"Nothing to fear," said Petronius. "Be over before you know it. Then you'll see how the Old Cats celebrate a victory."

From the moment the craft scraped the pebbly beach, Jason was caught up in the mass of legionaries jumping over the side, splashing to higher ground. The Britons swarmed down the cliffs, yelling savagely. Jason stumbled on the rocks, clutched at Gareth, then raced ahead, trying to keep up with Petronius and the Old Cats.

Arrows sang through the air. The legionaries hurled their spears. Howling and shrieking, the Britons poured across the beach. Then something Jason had never seen before appeared: small, rickety chariots darting in and out of the clusters of men. Drivers reined up the shaggy ponies; warriors leaped down, attacked sharply, and raced back. In a flash the drivers wheeled and the ponies galloped away. Even the well-trained legionaries could barely hold their ground against them. A wedge of shouting Britons cut Jason off from the Old Cats.

Holding Gareth under the cloak, Jason dashed farther down the beach to circle around and rejoin the Company. But the Britons covered that part of the ground and Jason found himself forced toward a fringe of scrubby trees.

A Briton charioteer sighted him, spun his pony, and began pursuit. Jason scrambled higher up the bank, plunging into the woods, running blindly, going deeper and deeper. Branches whipped his face. A root tripped him and he sprawled on the damp leaves.

"We're lost," Jason gasped. "We'll never get back to the Company."

Gareth sprang to the low limb of a tree. "I can track our

way out," he said. He stood motionless, his head cocked a little to one side. "But not now. They're still fighting on the beach," he said. "We'd better wait until after dark."

Catching his breath, Jason collapsed on a boulder. "I don't care what Petronius says. It's a lot quieter being an artichoke. And as far as being a mascot goes . . ." He stopped short. Gareth had begun to bristle. From the corner of his eye, Jason saw another animal crouching near the tree.

It looked very much like a cat, but a little bigger than Gareth, with long, shaggy hair. Its eyes were round and bright yellow; its body gray and stripy; tufts grew from the tips of its ears. The animal began a long whine, ending with a snarling, toothy kind of cough. Then it leaped.

Gareth grappled with the animal in mid-air. Two bodies thrashed on the ground and turned into a spinning, spitting ball. One screamed—Jason could not tell which. Locked to his opponent, Gareth rolled into the bushes. Jason ran to the spot as both animals crashed into the woods. He could hear the ripping of leaves.

"Gareth!" he cried.

Jason forced his way through the bushes, then flung himself back against a tree. In front of him stood a bearded man dressed in skins. He held a long, ugly spear pointed at Jason's throat.

5.
Cerdic Longtooth

The bearded man looked as frightened as Jason; but, since he was the one with the spear, Jason could only do as he ordered. The Briton cautiously stepped up to the tree and gestured for the boy to move away from it.

They headed deeper into the forest. Soon the path widened. Ahead lay a clearing, in its center a log enclosure banked with earth. A gate of logs opened so that the Briton and Jason could enter the village. It was mainly a row of huts, something like beehives of twigs and mud. Inside, Jason's captor shook his spear in the air and shouted triumphantly.

Other men wrapped in shaggy skins ran into the rutted street. Some hungry-looking dogs immediately began yelping and barking. By the time Jason reached the largest hut, the whole village was following at his heels.

A tall warrior with reddish hair down to his shoulders came out of the hut and stood with his arms folded across his chest. A handsome silver collarpiece hung at his throat. An enormous red mustache drooped under his bony nose and made his face appear very warlike and very melancholy at the same time. The man with the spear raised his voice:

"Cerdic Longtooth! Mighty chieftain! Know that I, Osric, with my bare hands captured this ignorant and highly dangerous savage!

"All day we struggled! Never was there such a battle!" Osric went on, stamping up and down, brandishing his spear. "Sorely wounded, still I fought on. At last, his natural cowardice betrayed him and I conquered. O great is Osric! Mighty is Osric!"

Jason, wretched with the dampness, exhausted from the march, finally lost his patience. "That's not true," he cried. "We didn't struggle all day. There wasn't any struggle at all. He jumped out at me with that spear. And I'm not ignorant and I'm not a savage!"

Another warrior stepped up and whispered something in the chieftain's ear. Longtooth nodded glumly, then raised his head and pointed his mustache at Jason.

"There's a question come up," Longtooth said. "Usually, when we catch somebody from beyond the woods, we simply chop them up. But you're an invader, and some of us have suggested it might be more correct to burn you in a basket. I rather agree. Osric, go fetch the basket."

From the hut a woman in a coarsely woven robe appeared, pushed Longtooth aside and shook her finger at him. "You'll do nothing of the kind, Cerdic Longtooth. I don't care who he is; he's only a boy and he's chilled to the bone. You bring him inside right away. Now march!"

She took Jason by the shoulders and led him through the door into a room where a fire of twigs billowed out smoke.

Cerdic Longtooth followed, grumbling loudly. "He's supposed to plead for his life now," the chieftain said. "That's the next step. I don't see why you have to interfere with these things. There's a right way and a wrong way."

"Pack of nonsense," the woman said. "He may be a foreigner and a savage, but that's not his fault and I'm quite sure he's done no harm."

While she rubbed Jason with a dry cloth, she directed a continuous stream of talk at her husband. If Longtooth would ever look farther than his nose, she said, he would see this was a good chance to have a slave young enough to train.

"Enough, woman, enough," Longtooth cried, holding his head. "I'll speak to the Druid about it in the morning. If he says we can keep the savage, we'll keep him."

Mrs. Longtooth agreed, and it was decided to lock Jason in the storeroom for the night. Mrs. Longtooth gave him a pot of stewed meat and an animal skin. Cerdic, acting as though Jason might attack him at any moment, pushed him into the dark room and jammed the door shut.

Jason flung himself on the ground, too exhausted even to think of trying to escape. Then he felt a soft paw on his arm and heard a familiar trill of recognition.

"Gareth! Are you all right?"

"Not so loud," warned the cat, hopping onto Jason's lap. "Yes, I'm fine. Couple of scratches, a little fur lost here and there. I've been through worse."

"What was that terrible animal?" Jason asked. "I've never seen one like it."

"A wildcat," Gareth said. "The only kind of cat they have here."

"What a fighter," Jason said. "I was afraid he might . . ."

"*She,*" said Gareth. "And she was frightened, more than anything else. It was quite a scuffle until she realized both of us were cats, and she apologized afterward. Then we got along very well. She told me about Longtooth's tribe. I got here faster than you did, and climbed through a broken place in the roof."

"Is there any way we can get out?" asked Jason.

"I could scratch open that roof some more," Gareth said. "But we wouldn't be any better off. We'd never get to the beach in time. You see," he added, "the Romans are leaving."

"The Old Cats? Everybody?" Jason swallowed hard. "What can we do now?"

"We'll have to stay here somehow," Gareth said.

"Do you think they'll let us? Longtooth's wife was very kind and wants to keep me for a slave, but Longtooth wants to burn me in a basket. The Druid, whoever that is, is going to decide. And what about you? Will you live in the woods?"

"I might not have to," said Gareth. "These Britons are like big children. They make up stories about things. The way they'd *like* them to happen. Whether they really happened that way doesn't matter. And I think that might help us. But we'll talk about it in the morning."

Jason and Gareth made themselves as comfortable as they could on the animal skin, pressing close to one another for warmth. This, Jason decided, was the dampest place he had ever been in. He couldn't imagine why it ever interested the Romans. And he thought sadly of all the Company, of Petronius, Arrius, the friends he would never meet again.

Next morning, Gareth had just finished telling Jason his plan when the storeroom door opened. Cerdic Longtooth peered in. Behind him stood his wife and a white-haired, white-bearded man in a long robe. As soon as Longtooth caught sight of Gareth, sitting on Jason's shoulder, the warrior tumbled back and bellowed, "Osric! Osric! Wild beasts! My spear!"

"Stop!" Jason shouted. "Know that I, Jason, have conquered the blackest, fiercest animal in Britain! Great is my power over him! See his claws, his teeth! Yet I touch him without harm!"

Jason held out an arm toward Longtooth. Gareth slowly walked down the arm and stopped, perched there. The cat raised his head and stared with orange eyes at the warrior.

"All night we struggled," Jason went on. "Great is the power of Jason!"

"I can believe that," said the Druid, craning his neck to see past Longtooth. "It's a very ferocious-looking animal. Something like those catamountains in the woods—and you can't even get near *them*. Amazing. The savage does seem to have a kind of power over it."

"What I want to know, Druid," said Longtooth, "is this animal good luck or bad?"

"Some of our best families, you know," the Druid said, "pray to the spirit of the catamountain. But this is the first time anyone has ever been, shall we say, visited by one. So I should think it would be very good luck, that is, so long as the animal behaves itself."

"Druid," said Longtooth, "I would like to make you a present of this lucky animal. You can have its keeper, too."

"Well, really," the Druid answered, "I appreciate your thought. But my duties in the tribe take up so much time. No, Longtooth, as our war leader it would be more proper for you to look after them both. As a matter of fact, I give you the official responsibility. It's quite an honor, Longtooth, to have such an animal."

"Yes," Longtooth said glumly. "I rather thought you'd see it that way."

Cerdic Longtooth looked more melancholy than ever. Mrs. Longtooth, on the other hand, was delighted.

Gareth, after investigating the hut, discovered that the place was overrun with mice. Within a week, the mice had vanished.

"A jewel!" Mrs. Longtooth cried. "This catamountain's a jewel! I'm not surprised the Druid called him lucky. Why, I'd have lost half our winter stores without him!"

Word spread that Longtooth's ferocious black animal was protecting their food. Each day, at least half-a-dozen visitors stopped by to admire Gareth—from a safe distance. Even the Druid himself came to call. After that, Cerdic began watching Gareth with pride.

One evening, Jason happened to find a length of cord. He pulled it across the dirt floor while Gareth romped after the end, rolling over, batting the string with his paws.

"What's he doing that for?" asked Cerdic.

"Just for fun," Jason said. "He's playing. He does it to keep in practice, too."

Longtooth got up and walked cautiously toward the cat. "He's a quick one, isn't he?" Then, hesitantly, he added, "Do you think he'd do it with me?"

"You could try," Jason said.

The Briton knelt on the floor and picked up the cord. Gareth pounced at it and Cerdic began to laugh, as gleeful as a child.

From then on, Cerdic could hardly wait for another chance to play with Gareth. Each evening after dinner, the warrior would pick up the cord and call the cat. When the cord wore out, Cerdic unfastened his own collarpiece and dragged the chain along the ground.

Still, Cerdic had never gotten up the courage to touch Gareth. Although he had often seen the cat sit on Jason's lap, Longtooth insisted it was dangerous.

"It isn't dangerous at all," Jason said. "Here . . ."

Before the warrior could protest, Jason lifted Gareth to Cerdic's knees.

Cerdic sat rigidly, not daring to move. "He's making a noise," the warrior said nervously. "I think he's getting ready to bite."

"He's purring," Jason said. "That means he's pleased and he likes you."

"Likes me?" Longtooth said hopefully. "Do you really think so?"

In answer, Gareth stretched up his neck and rubbed his head against the warrior's mustache.

"By the Druid's beard!" Cerdic cried. "I believe he *does* like me!"

The tall warrior, smiling, held Gareth on his lap and stroked him until it was time for them all to go to sleep.

Winter came early. The snow drifted high and the village settled in on itself. Jason had almost grown used to the climate, and he found the hut snug and cozy—even though Cerdic had never got round to fixing the hole in the store-room roof.

Once, Jason thought he caught a glimpse of the wild-cat.

"Yes, she's out there," Gareth said, when he and Jason were alone. "She's terribly hungry, too."

Jason promised to save some meat from his dinner and put it near the hut.

The white days passed quietly. Mrs. Longtooth looked after the hut, with Jason often giving her a hand (she had quite forgotten that he was supposed to be a slave). Cerdic polished his weapons and, when he got through, began polishing them all over again. Often, Gareth would jump to Cerdic's lap and drowse there, and the warrior would beam happily.

One day, just before sundown, Mrs. Longtooth went to the storeroom. A moment later she flew back into the hut.

"A catamountain! There's another one!"

Cerdic, Jason, and Gareth ran to the storeroom. It was true. The wildcat lay curled on a heap of skins, and watched them with solemn yellow eyes. Only then did they notice she was not alone. Four tiny kittens nestled at her side.

"The poor thing," Mrs. Longtooth said. "It must have been so cold for her."

"Amazing," said Longtooth. "These catamountains don't look half as wild in here as they do outside." The warrior drew closer. The wildcat hissed a little, warning him away from the kittens. "Don't worry, old girl," said Longtooth. "You'll stay here as long as you please."

"And the little ones," Mrs. Longtooth exclaimed.

"They have their eyes shut so tight. Will they ever be as lucky as our animal?"

"They'll be fine," said Longtooth.

While Cerdic and his wife admired the kittens, Jason and Gareth walked quietly away.

"Do you really think they'll stay?" Jason asked.

"I believe so," Gareth said. "Oh, they'll never forget the wilds. No cat does. They may even go back now and again. But this is a new beginning for them."

The door of the hut had come unlatched and was standing half-open. Gareth went toward it. Jason glanced back to see Longtooth and his wife still bent over the new arrivals. The kittens, Jason remembered, were tawny, with dark stripes. All but one. And that one was black with a white mark on its chest.

Gareth, like a shadow, leaped onto the hard snow crust outside. Jason's shadow followed him.

Ireland

•

411 A.D.

6.
Diahan

They had left Britain far behind. Here, in Ireland, a girl stood on a cluster of rocks. Red-gold hair tossed about her shoulders, reaching the belt of gold at her waist. Behind her rose the hills, iron black, brine green. She was Jason's age, tall, slim, with tiny feet in sandals. The girl did not seem at all surprised; as soon as she noticed Jason and Gareth, she ran forward lightly, her blue eyes sparkling, and began talking as if she had no intention of stopping.

"My name is Diahan," she said a little breathlessly, in an accent more like singing than speaking. "What's yours?" Before Jason could answer, she hurried on. "My father is King Miliucc. Is your father a king? Would it be you, the son of King Mogh of the Mighty Arm? Then you must tell your father to send back all the cows, especially the red one —she's my favorite. If you don't, we'll come and take them and all of yours, too."

Without taking a breath, the girl bent and looked closely at Gareth. "But I never heard of Mogh having a dog like this. He must be no good at all against a wolf."

"He isn't afraid of wolves and he isn't a dog," Jason managed to interrupt. "He's a cat."

"A cat?" said Diahan. "Why, of course, he's a cat."

"Then why did you call him a dog?" Jason asked.

"I meant cat," Diahan said. "The other slipped out. Are you saying I wouldn't know a dog when I see one?"

"You may know what a dog is," said Jason, "but I don't think you're very sure about cats."

"It's not polite of you to say that." Diahan pursed her lips. But she could not resist talking again. "I don't think you're Mogh's boy at all, and that's not a cat at all."

"I'm not King Mogh's boy," said Jason. "I never told you I was. But this is a cat, no matter what you say."

Diahan stamped her foot. "I say you're a stupid boy. Everybody knows cats are bigger than that. The one that carried off Seanchan, the greatest poet in Erin, was big as an ox. That's what Dubthach says, and he's always right."

Jason sat down on the rock and began to laugh. "I don't know King Mogh or King Miliucc or Seanchan or Dubthach, but there's no cat in the world as big as an ox."

"Then if he wasn't as big as that, how could he carry off Seanchan? Dubthach is a poet, too, and he must know what happens to other poets."

Jason shook his head. "Cats don't carry off people. That's one thing they don't do."

Diahan put her hands on her hips and looked sharply at him. "If you're such a wise boy, tell me what they *can* do."

"They can climb trees and see in the dark," Jason said, "they can purr and catch rats and . . ."

"Catch rats?" said Diahan. "We have something better for rats. We have Lugad."

"What's a lugad?" asked Jason.

Diahan giggled. "Not *what's* a Lugad; *who's* a Lugad. Lugad is the magician at my father's court. All he needs to do is cast a spell, and the rats and all the creepy, crawly things go away. Or so he says. Can your cat work magic?"

"In a way . . ." Jason began.

Diahan brightened. "Of course! He could *wish* himself big as an ox. I knew Dubthach couldn't be wrong. Come now!"

She took Jason's hand and jumped from the rock.

"You must show your magic cat to my father," she said. "And especially to Lugad."

Diahan skipped in front of them all the way down the valley. Without Diahan as a guide, Jason was sure he would have walked right through the center of Miliucc's kingdom. He saw only a cluster of clay-and-wattle huts and a pen with four very thin pigs drowsing in it. A small herd of cows ambled by, driven by a young, dark-haired man with a staff.

"Sucat! Sucat!" called Diahan as soon as she spied the cowherd. "Here's something this boy calls a cat. Is it really one? You should know."

Catching sight of Gareth, the herdsman dropped to one knee and held out his hands. Jason, surprised, saw the cat bound ahead and jump to the man's lap. The herdsman put his cheek against Gareth's shoulder. "Yes, little princess, this is a cat. I've not seen one for six years, but I've not forgotten. And what," he asked with a smile, "did you make him out to be? One of your father's wolfhounds?"

"That's twice today I've been laughed at," Diahan pouted. "It's not my fault if I thought a cat should be bigger. Besides, he's a magic cat, he'll cast a spell and get big as an ox if you aren't careful."

The herdsman sighed and shook a finger gently at the girl. "Now, little princess, how many times have I told you? There are no magic beasts, only God's creatures as you see them, and no spells worth the saying of them."

Diahan toed the ground uneasily with the tip of her sandal. "I know that's what you say. But Lugad says . . ."

The man raised his head sharply and his eyes flashed. "Lugad is a porridge-headed fool!"

Diahan clapped a hand to her mouth. "That's a terrible thing to say." Then she giggled. "He does look like one, though. But I hope he never hears you call him that."

"Lugad doesn't frighten me." Sucat smiled. "Let him think about my name. In Britain, they called me Patrick. But my real name is Sucat. It means 'Good Cat'—and it means 'Good Warrior.' For in my land, the land of Wales," he added, "we call our warriors 'Cats.' "

"You come from Wales?" Jason asked. "But that must be far . . ."

"Far and across the water," Sucat said. He looked Jason up and down. "Something tells me you, too, are a stranger."

"We've come a long way," Jason said.

"Then we must talk, we two strangers," said Sucat. "And you must grant me the pleasure of holding that handsome cat on my knees. From what Princess Diahan says, you can guess with no trouble that this is not a land of cats. Although," he went on with a wry smile, "it is a land of many other things."

Watching Sucat, Jason had the feeling that this man, with his black hair and broad forehead, was only playing at being a cowherd. He was not big or heavily muscled, but Jason had seen fire in Sucat's eyes when he had spoken of

Lugad. In his face, the turn of his head, there had been a kind of power at rest—much the way Gareth looked when he was sleeping, with his legs stretched out, as limp as water —yet Jason knew Gareth could be on his feet in a moment, the springs of his lean body coiled tight and ready. Sucat, Jason thought, could do the same.

Diahan, who had been silent longer than any time since Jason had met her, finally interrupted.

"Enough chattering! All you want to do is talk and you don't give me a word for myself. And me the one who found the magic cat in the first place."

Diahan took Jason by the hand and led him away.

"If you want the truth," she said, "Lugad is a porridge-head. My father isn't pleased with him at all. Oh, Lugad is very clever at big things—making the sun come up at his command and all that. But he really isn't good at the small ones. The village is still full of rats and snakes.

"Of course, Lugad says they're just the *spirits* of the rats and snakes; he says he got rid of the real ones long ago. I don't know," Diahan shook her head. "There's not a season passes that they don't ruin half our stores. If they're spirits— wisha! They have marvelous great appetites. They eat as much as the real ones!"

Inside a tall, raftered house, with bronze decorations at the gates, Diahan presented Jason to her father, a barrel-chested, red-bearded warrior with gold ornaments on his arms and a royal cloak of seven colors over his bare shoulders. The lean, quizzical-looking man holding a harp was the poet Dubthach, Jason guessed. There could be no mistaking Lugad, a heavy, waddling fellow, completely bald, with eyes like sour blueberries.

When Diahan told King Miliucc that Jason and his cat were magicians, the warrior slapped the table. "That's what we need," he cried. "Some new magic from afar. Sometimes, I'm thinking, your spells are a little worn at the edges, Lugad."

The court magician twiddled his fingers and muttered in a peculiar way. Jason didn't know whether or not it was a spell, but it sounded very insulting.

King Miliucc gave Jason and Gareth the hospitality which custom demanded for any stranger, especially two wandering magicians. Jason's room in the palace had a great bed and soft feather cushions. But that night, Jason could not settle himself. Diahan's talk of spells, of cats as big as oxen kept running through his mind; as well as the red-gold hair of Diahan herself.

Restless, Jason and Gareth quietly left the room and strolled through the silver moonlight to the edge of the village, to the fringe of gnarled trees that bent and twisted like ancient magicians dancing.

"But who are these people?" Jason asked. "They remind me a little of Cerdic Longtooth and the Druid, except they know how to make things better. Cerdic would have loved a few of King Miliucc's armbands."

"You're right, in a way," said Gareth. "These Irish have their own kind of druids, and they've been here for thousands of years. The story goes that there was a wild warrior people living north of Greece. They were just a small part of an enormous tribe called the Celts, and they moved down and stayed with the Egyptians for a while; then they went to Spain; and, finally, ended up on this island. Other people were living here, but the Celtic warriors drove them off;

they still think their spirits live under the hills. They call them the Little People."

"Were there any cats?"

"No," Gareth said. "The warriors got to know about cats long ago in Egypt. But they never had any of their own. They've forgotten what a real cat is like so they've made up fairy tales about them. It's a way of remembering."

"They certainly remembered wrong," Jason laughed.

Something in the pool of moonlight caught Gareth's attention. Without another word he slid forward. Perhaps it was a cricket or a beetle, Jason could not tell; perhaps Gareth was only practicing again. But the cat leaped high in the pale silver beams. The night dew sparkled around him. Here, at the edge of the gnarled trees, with Gareth dancing like a wild, mysterious creature, Jason could almost see the Little People of Erin rising from the grass to watch. As Gareth's sinewy body turned, as the moon flickered white in the cat's eyes, Jason, in spite of himself, shivered with a delightful kind of scariness.

When the cat finished his game, or his hunting practice, he padded back to Jason. Neither spoke. The spell of the land of Erin hung over both of them, like cobwebs of gold. In silence, they walked slowly back to King Miliucc's palace. Jason once glanced behind him, half-expecting to see a band of Little People following them.

A scream broke the spell. It was Diahan's voice. Jason raced through the empty hall to the sleeping chambers. Gareth bounded ahead of him. Diahan was sitting upright in the low bed, her eyes wide with terror.

In the center of the floor, cold moonlight like a sheet of ice over its scales, a serpent was poised, ready to strike.

7.
Sucat

Jason froze where he stood. The only movement in the room was the black arrow of Gareth leaping forward. Before the serpent could strike, Gareth caught it behind its flat skull. The serpent's tail lashed out and wound around Gareth's body. Over and over, the fighters rolled across the floor. Gareth was on his back now, his hind paws furiously kicking.

Once, the serpent tried to raise itself as if to smash the cat against the floor. Gareth hung on with tooth and claw. The serpent thrashed a circle around the chamber. Jason caught his breath as he saw Gareth tumble head over tail. For an instant the serpent almost shook itself free, but Gareth still gripped its neck.

Suddenly, it was over. The serpent went lifeless as a piece of rope. Even then, Gareth did not loosen his jaws. With eyes blazing, he crouched, moaning and growling. As Jason saw him at that moment, Gareth was a wild creature of the forest once again, a creature of slashing claws and sharp teeth, victorious over a deadly enemy.

Torchlight flooded the room. In the doorway stood

King Miliucc, his red hair flying about his head, a sword in his fist. Behind him crowded the palace guard. Diahan, who had been too frightened even to whimper during the fight, burst into tears.

While King Miliucc comforted the sobbing Diahan, Jason ran toward Gareth. The cat shook himself from his shoulders down to the tip of his tail, then blinked up at Jason.

Gareth dropped the serpent with a disdainful toss of his head. Very calmly, he began to wash.

Still puffy with sleep, looking more like a porridge than ever, Lugad rolled into the chamber. "What's this?" he asked. "A nightmare? Is that all? The girl's been sleeping in the moonlight."

"Nightmare!" roared Miliucc, picking up the limp body of the serpent and thrusting it at Lugad. "I'll nightmare you! Do you call this moonlight?"

Lugad glanced at the serpent distastefully. "An evil spirit," he said. "An evil spirit if I ever saw one."

King Miliucc turned redder than his hair. "Wisha, man! If I wrapped this around your neck and pulled a little, you'd not call it a spirit!"

"This is the ghost of a serpent," said Lugad peevishly, looking down his nose at Miliucc and at the same time moving away a little—just in case the King had any intention of carrying out his threat. "I don't know how many times I have to tell you. I have driven the real ones away."

"Then," cried Miliucc, "you mean to say, standing there with your great bald head, that a daughter of mine has been in danger of her life from the bite of a ghost?"

Lugad shrugged. "That's the way of it with ghosts. But

pay it no mind. I'll put a spell on the chamber. She'll have no more danger this night."

"Cast your spells on the wind," shouted Miliucc, "for all the good they do. Why, this little black cat here has more power in one whisker than you have in that barrel of fat!"

"Beware!" Lugad raised his hand in the air. " 'Tis death to mock a magician!"

"True," said Miliucc, with a sour grin. "But if you're as much magician as I think you are, I'll have no fear!"

Lugad snorted, turned on his heel, and pushed his way out of the chamber.

King Miliucc turned to Jason and Gareth. "You two shall sit at my right hand," he said. "The finest smith in Erin shall make thrones of silver for you. The harp of Dubthach shall sing of a magician greater than Lugad!"

Next day, Miliucc indeed seated Jason and Gareth on silver thrones. Dubthach sang song after song of praise. Diahan looked at Jason admiringly, while Lugad, banished to the far end of the table in the draughts and smoke, muttered angrily to himself.

That was not all. The red-bearded King asked Jason and Gareth to stay and be his court magicians.

"But we can't . . ." Jason began. "You don't understand. . . ."

"Wisha!" cried Miliucc. "I understand magic when I see it! It's settled, then!" He turned away and would listen to none of Jason's protests.

After the meal, as they were leaving the hall, Diahan came to walk beside Jason. "I heard what my father said," she whispered excitedly. "Isn't it wonderful? You'll be much better than Lugad. His magic is so weary and dreary."

"You don't understand either," Jason said in despair. "I'm not a magician and neither is Gareth."

"You said he was."

"Yes, but not the kind you mean. I can't explain any more."

"Of course, of course." Diahan nodded knowingly. "It's not wise for a magician to boast of his skill. The Little People might hear and be jealous."

"It isn't the Little People . . ."

"Sst! Sst!" Diahan put a finger to Jason's lips. "Don't mention their name or we'll have a plague of them!"

"I'm not worried about that," Jason said. "I'm worried about what to tell your father. He just won't listen to me."

"If you refuse," Diahan warned, "he'll be furious. And for the matter of that, so will I." She flashed her eyes at him. "If you won't be court magician instead of that silly Lugad, I'll not speak to you again!"

Jason left Diahan at the palace. Still wondering what to tell Miliucc, he made his way to the cow pen to find Sucat.

The Welshman was sitting on the top rail of the enclosure. He waved at the boy, bent down, and picked up Gareth and held him in his lap. Sucat listened carefully while Jason told him the problem.

"I think you're right," Sucat said. "There can be only trouble if you or your cat start playing magician. Better leave all that business to Lugad."

"But didn't you say his spells are useless?" Jason asked.

"His spells are," Sucat agreed, "but not his knowledge. The thing you must understand about these magicians is this: they really know a great deal. They know the stars, how to figure the seasons; they know farming and planting, all the ways of the woods and animals. Some of them can even put a man to sleep just by looking him in the eye. The trouble comes when they try to pretend that they work by magic instead of by nature.

"Lugad isn't all fool," Sucat went on. "He wants people to believe in the magic part of what he does, because then they'll stay afraid of him. It's a way of keeping his job, and you can't blame him too much. It's a shame, though. If he'd been living in Britain, now, he might have made a fine, learned man. We have the Christian faith in my land and he could have had an education from the church, as I did. But there is none of that in Erin, only magic and superstition and the Little People under every blade of grass. No," Sucat sighed, "this is far from Britain."

"If Britain is civilized now," Jason asked, "why did you come here?"

"Come?" Sucat smiled sadly. "I did not come, boy; I was taken. I shall always remember the night King Niall of the Nine Hostages raided our coast.

"There were three of us in the house: my two sisters and me. They took us all, to sell as slaves. Oh, I was a fighter in those days, but they were too many. They tied us up, carried us to the boat, and sailed away.

"My sisters are in Erin, somewhere," Sucat continued. "I pray they still live. Miliucc bought me to herd his cows. That was six years ago."

"Why don't you escape?" asked Jason. "They never seem to lock you up."

"When the time comes," Sucat said, "I may go from this place. But look you, this idea is in my mind: that underneath it all there is some purpose, some reason I should be here. What it may be is hidden from me now. When I understand it, perhaps then I shall go, or perhaps I shall stay."

The herdsman was silent after that, his face lost in a dream, his deep-set eyes looking far past Jason toward the hills.

Finally, Jason spoke. "I still don't know what to do about Miliucc."

"The King?" said Sucat. "Oh, as far as that goes, do nothing at all. Miliucc changes his mind from one moment to the next, and he doesn't remember half of what he says. Right now he's angry at Lugad because of the serpent. But Miliucc always agrees with the last person who talks to him. Lugad is a clever one; he'll work him around. So my advice is just stay out of it and he'll forget the whole thing."

Sucat, Jason realized, was quite right. In the hall, at the next meal, Lugad had his old place at the table. The magician and the King talked earnestly back and forth, paying no attention to anyone else. Diahan was so annoyed at Jason's letting his opportunity slip that she refused to speak to him, except to remind him, several times, that she wasn't speaking to him.

Lugad busied himself with preparations for the Midsummer Fires, ordering parties of men to carry straw and wood to the mountaintop. The Fires, Jason learned, were supposed to guarantee a good harvest for the village. A lot of spells had to be cast over them, and Lugad was making a very grand thing of it. Jason and Gareth were completely forgotten.

"You see what I mean?" Sucat asked, when Jason spoke

to him again. "There's no need of magic fires for a good crop. If the farmers plant their seed as they should and the weather holds, the harvest will be good. If not . . ." Sucat shrugged. "No fire on earth can help them. If they'd pay more attention to the rats that eat their grain," he went on, "they'd be better off."

"Gareth could help with the rats," Jason said. "He's done it every place he's been and he's very good at it."

"There's only one of him," Sucat said. "A hundred cats would hardly be enough. Every village in Erin has the same trouble, and it can only get worse. There will soon be famines and starvation such as no man can remember. Then what good will Lugad and his fires be?"

Jason agreed. But that night, when the fires were lit, he also had to admit he had never seen such a blaze. The whole mountaintop flamed. Jason, Sucat, and Gareth perched on the cow-pen railing to watch the ragged sheets of orange scorch the black night. Soon, the fires of neighboring villages appeared on other hilltops.

The fires had hardly begun when Jason saw Diahan running toward the pen. Her face was scratched with brambles, her white robe torn. Sucat jumped down and hurried to meet her.

"Little princess," he called, "I thought you were in the hills with your father."

"I was," Diahan gasped. "But I had to get away. It's terrible what they're going to do. It was Lugad's idea . . ." She began to sob.

Sucat took her by the shoulders. "Calm yourself, girl. What's this you say about Lugad?"

"He's been talking to my father," Diahan said. "Lugad

still says all the serpents and rats are ghosts . . . and he says the only way to get rid of them is to send another ghost after them."

"I should have known Lugad would think of something like that," Sucat said angrily.

"He wants to send two ghosts." Diahan's lips trembled. "The ghosts of a boy—and a cat!"

"I don't need to guess who that boy and cat might be," Sucat said grimly.

Diahan turned to Jason. "You must go. You dare not wait. Lugad's coming down now with his men. They want to wrap you both up in leaves and throw you in the fire.

"Sucat," she hurried on, "you must show them the path through the woods. Quickly! And you must not come back. If Lugad ever found out you helped them escape, he'd have you killed."

"But what about you, little princess?" the herdsman asked.

"I am my father's daughter," said Diahan proudly. "Lugad would not dare to harm me. Only hurry! It will be too late!"

Diahan took Jason's arm. "Farewell to you, boy—and that dog, or cat, or whatever you call it." The princess hastily kissed him on the cheek. As she lowered her eyes, Jason saw tears on the long lashes. "I didn't mean what I said about not speaking to you," Diahan whispered. "And I am not happy to see you go."

By dawn, Jason, Gareth, and Sucat were well into the forest and far beyond the reach of Lugad. They had walked most of the night in silence. Sucat had been wrapped in his own thoughts; and Jason, to his surprise, found himself missing the golden-haired Diahan.

Sucat was the first to speak.

"It is a curious thing," he said, "but I have come to love this country, even as a slave. Perhaps that was the reason for my captivity, that I should learn to know Erin and its people and to love them. I understand now what I must do.

"I shall go into the world," Sucat went on, "perhaps even as far as Rome itself. I shall learn and bring back what I learn. There shall be no need for magicians then."

"What about the serpents? And the rats?" asked Jason.

"The serpents of war and ignorance are worse than those that creep along the ground," Sucat said. "These serpents are the ones I shall drive out. And as far as the rats are concerned . . ." He smiled, reached down, and patted Gareth. "I shall bring some of these little creatures with me."

The travelers stopped in a clearing. Striking a flint, Sucat made a small fire of twigs. "Rest now," he said. "We have a long journey."

The Welshman stretched out beside the fire and soon fell asleep. Still wakeful, Jason and Gareth wandered toward the fringe of trees.

"It's strange," Jason said, "the way Sucat was talking. He made me think of someone else . . . it was a saint. . . ."

"Someone else?" Gareth said. "No. There's only one man like Sucat. Don't you remember, Sucat told you he had another name? It's Patrick."

The fire burned out. From the embers one last flame and a wisp of smoke rose to the sunlight.

Japan

·

998 A.D.

8.
Master of Imperial Cats

"Come! Enter quickly!"

Jason blinked his eyes. Only an instant before he and Gareth had been in a forest of Erin. Now, in a street in Japan, an old man with a wispy mustache and narrow white beard was calling to them from a sedan chair.

"Enter! Enter!" insisted the old man, whose face was the color of a very pale lemon. He seized Jason by the wrist and pulled him in. From the outside, the sedan chair looked like a fancy box carried between two poles; inside, Jason felt he was riding in a tiny, spicy-smelling cabin.

"Forgive this humble personage," said the man, who introduced himself as Sun-Cheng, "but it surprised me to see a cat in the Imperial City. There aren't any more, are there?" he asked anxiously.

"I don't know," Jason said. "We just got here ourselves. But I haven't seen any."

Sun-Cheng pulled a little paper fan from his embroidered sleeve and began fanning himself rapidly. "What a relief! I had promised the Emperor Ichigo something that could not be found in all Japan. And with emperors," he added, "promise nothing you can't deliver."

As they jogged along, Sun-Cheng explained that he was a merchant and trader. He himself was not Japanese but Chinese, and journeyed to Kyoto, the Imperial City, once a year. "The Emperor is never satisfied," Sun-Cheng went on. "Always something new." He shook his head. "This time," he said, pointing to a large, red lacquered box with holes in the lid, "it will truly be a most honorable surprise. You could oblige this useless one if you would come along—as a sample of merchandise."

Jason didn't see how he or Gareth could be "samples," but he agreed to stay with the merchant.

The sedan chair entered the palace grounds. Every few minutes Sun-Cheng had to thrust a rice paper scroll out the narrow window of the sedan chair so the guards would let them pass. They stopped in front of the palace. Sun-Cheng, clutching his red box, hustled out. Jason, with Gareth in his arms, followed the old Chinese up a wide flight of steps. A crowd of chamberlains, major-domos, and imperial servants hurried them down the corridors so quickly that Jason barely had time to look around. He only glimpsed the richly embroidered draperies, the painted screens, the great lanterns. Guards stood everywhere, stiff and motionless, in shining armor, holding spears and wicked-looking swords.

Approaching the door to the Emperor's throne room, Sun-Cheng began to tremble. "Do what I do," he whispered. "It will cost your humble, worthless head if you don't."

In front of the massive door Sun-Cheng threw himself to his knees and bowed his head until it touched the floor. Jason did the same. "Don't look up," Sun-Cheng whispered.

A gong crashed and the doors were flung open. Sun-Cheng began crawling forward, his head low. From the corner of one eye, Jason saw more ranks of guards. He inched ahead. The throne room seemed a mile long.

"These are two unworthy and totally useless specks of dust," one of the chamberlains cried. "They seek a precious moment of the Imperial Majesty's celestial and incredibly valuable time."

Another gong crashed and Jason's ears began to sing. Still on his knees, wringing his hands, Sun-Cheng at last raised his head. Jason, too, straightened up. They were almost at the foot of the throne where sat the Emperor Ichigo. He wore so many kimonos, sashes, and layer after layer of stiff, gold-threaded skirts that he looked like a doll.

The Emperor Ichigo was a boy, no older than Jason.

Sun-Cheng fumbled with his lacquered box, pulled off the lid, and turned the box on its side. Out rolled five brown-and-black striped kittens.

Mewing, blinking, the kittens seemed about to run off in all directions; but catching sight of Gareth, they clustered around him. The black cat gave each of them a few reassuring licks.

Ichigo clapped his hands with delight and jumped off the throne. In another moment he was on the floor beside Jason and Gareth, peering at the kittens with amazement and fascination.

"I want them!" he exclaimed. "What are they?"

"These are what we call cats, Imperial Highness," Sun-Cheng explained. "In our humble land they are ancient and honorable creatures."

"Why are there two sizes?" Ichigo asked.

"The small ones are young," Sun-Cheng said. "In time, they will grow."

"Cats," Ichigo whispered with a smile. "I think that's what I've always wanted."

Jason had been so busy looking at the kittens playing around Gareth that he did not notice a man in glistening armor who stood just behind Ichigo. With his hands on his hips, he scowled down at the Emperor.

"What is this nonsense?" he asked, in a voice like a whip.

Ichigo turned to him. "Oh, Uncle Fujiwara, please let me keep them."

The man gave the kittens a scornful glance. "They don't look as if they'd taste very good."

"Honorable Regent," Sun-Cheng cried, bowing and bumping his head against the floor, "Exalted guide and instructor of the Celestial Emperor, kittens are not to be eaten. They are far too precious."

"Then, miserable worm, what good are they?"

"Observe their eyes," Sun-Cheng said. "You can tell the time of day as they grow from narrow to wide. They will predict the weather for you when they wash themselves in a certain way. They will sing melodious songs, they will dance. . . ."

"Don't forget mice," Jason whispered.

"Sh!" the trader fearfully whispered back. "We don't talk about mice in the Imperial Palace."

"Please, Uncle, please," Ichigo begged. The boy bowed his own head before the Regent. "I never ask you for very much. . . ."

"Who will take charge of these animals?" asked the

Regent. "Trader, if you provide a keeper for them, perhaps I shall let them remain with the Emperor."

Sun-Cheng began to protest that he had urgent business in China; otherwise he would be delighted.

The Regent shrugged. "Then take your cats back."

Ichigo, hearing this, looked so unhappy that Jason quickly spoke up.

"My cat and I will stay with the kittens."

Ichigo brightened instantly. "You shall be Master of Imperial Cats," he ordered. "I grant you all the privileges of the Imperial Household—if Uncle Fujiwara agrees."

The Regent grudgingly nodded. "Now I suppose we must discuss your price." He gestured brusquely and Sun-Cheng crawled backward out of the throne room, the Regent striding after him. The two boys sat and looked at each other for a moment. Jason was not sure how to address a divine emperor. But now that the Regent was gone, Ichigo took off his imperial headdress and tossed it on the floor. He grinned at Jason. "I'm glad Uncle Fujiwara let me keep them. I don't know what I'd have done if you hadn't said you'd stay."

"I always thought emperors did as they pleased," said Jason.

Ichigo shook his head sadly. "Not with Uncle Fujiwara around. Of course," he added, "perhaps all emperors don't have an Uncle Fujiwara." He picked up one of the kittens and held it in his cupped hands. The little animal wrapped his forepaws around Ichigo's thumb and playfully nibbled his fingers. "Now," Ichigo said, "the first thing you must do is teach them etiquette. Otherwise, Uncle Fujiwara will be very displeased."

"Etiquette?" Jason asked. "Don't worry about that. Cats are always well behaved—most always, anyway."

"No, no," said Ichigo. "They must learn the Imperial Obeisance. Everybody does it when they come into the throne room, except Uncle, of course."

"You mean all that bowing and creeping?" Jason said. He almost laughed out loud until he saw, from the boy's solemn expression, that Ichigo was very serious about it.

"Oh yes," said the Emperor. "That's what you have to do when you approach the Celestial Presence—that's me."

"Well, I'm afraid that no cat in the world ever bowed to an emperor," said Jason. "They just won't do it, Ichigo, and you're wasting your time if you try to force them. A cat does what he wants, when he wants, emperor or not."

Ichigo thought for a moment. "Very well, Master of Imperial Cats," he said. "If you say so." Then he sighed. "They must be proud creatures. Even prouder than an emperor," he added wistfully.

"What I think you should do first," Jason said, "is feed them."

"Food? Ah so! Of course we must feed them." Without looking up or even turning around, Ichigo clapped his hands twice. "Bring food! The finest delicacies in the palace!"

To Jason's amazement, a minute later fourteen servants marched in. They knelt, bumped their heads on the floor, and then brought forward an array of covered dishes, bowls, saucers—and a dozen pairs of tiny chopsticks. The covers were whisked away revealing beautifully polished fruits, raisins, sweetmeats, decorated cookies, preserves.

"Oh, no!" Jason cried. "There's nothing here a cat can

eat! Ichigo, tell them to bring some plain food—meat or fish or a little milk."

Ichigo clapped his hands again and the servants disappeared. He looked so forlorn and disappointed that Jason, forgetting for a moment that Ichigo was a Celestial Presence, put a hand on the boy's shoulder.

"Don't feel bad, Ichigo," Jason said. "There's a lot to know about cats, and you have to start somewhere."

Later, after everyone had been properly fed, a procession of servants led Jason, Gareth, and the kittens to their sleeping quarters in another wing of the palace. There the walls were made of sliding paper screens, opened to the gentle night air. The scent of flowers filled the room; in the moonlight, across the Imperial grounds, Jason saw garden after garden and rows of blossoming cherry trees, and heard the rustle of a miniature waterfall. Throughout the gardens the breeze stirred hanging bamboo rods which gave a melodious, woodeny kind of ring. Crickets chirped in tiny wicker cages.

"You know," Jason said, "after Ireland and Britain, this is quite a change."

"The Japanese have had this for centuries," Gareth said. "And the Chinese civilization, for that matter, is even older. They had books and science and beautiful buildings when Cerdic Longtooth and his friends were shivering in their huts."

"But I still have the feeling," Jason went on, "that Ichigo really doesn't know what's happening outside the throne room. The way he ordered dinner, for example. He just clapped his hands and the food appeared. I don't think it ever occurred to him that people had to get it ready, real people that is, and real cats had to eat it."

"I'm afraid most emperors act that way," Gareth said. "Remember Neter-Khet in Egypt? Well, we cats don't care whether a person calls himself a Pharaoh or a Celestial Presence; he's still a man as far as we're concerned. But it can make a lot of difference to the humans who have to put up with him.

"The truth is," Gareth went on, "the more an emperor knows about his people, and about his own job, the better off he is. Neter-Khet at least knew he was a ruler. Poor Ichigo doesn't even know that. He has a lot to learn. Then again, so do these kittens," Gareth added, "but I'll look after that in the morning."

Next day, however, Gareth had little opportunity to do so. Ichigo had summoned to the throne room thirty-seven artists, nineteen poets, forty-two scholars, and, to create a soothing atmosphere, eighty-three musicians. The artists painted pictures of the kittens; the scholars examined them, and each scholar disagreed completely as to exactly what kind of an animal a cat was; and the musicians played on flutes, beat on drums, tapped blocks of wood, and plucked instruments that looked like banjos with most of the strings missing.

There was such a racket of music, arguments, comings and goings, creeping and bowing that Gareth flattened his ears against the noise and switched his tail irritably. The kittens, terrified, hid under Ichigo's throne and refused to come out.

"Ichigo," Jason said, "as Master of Imperial Cats I have to advise you to send all these people away."

"But they only come to admire," Ichigo protested.

"It doesn't matter," said Jason firmly. "Cats don't mind being admired if you do it sort of one at a time. And I think there's been enough admiring already. Besides, the kittens have a lot of important work to do."

Ichigo looked disappointed again; but since Uncle Fujiwara wasn't there, he followed Jason's advice. He clapped his hands, and a few seconds later the room was empty. The kittens one by one poked out their heads and Gareth finally persuaded them to come from under the throne.

With only Jason and Ichigo watching, the kittens frolicked about the room, tumbling over the polished floors. Gareth, who had been sitting quietly, slid forward slowly until he became a long black shadow amid the tiny balls of black-and-brown fur.

The kittens raced toward the older cat. Gareth rolled to his side. Hind legs pumping, he tossed each attacking kitten in the air. The little ones pounced for his tail. Gareth kept it out of reach, pulling it away just in time. While the kittens scuffled with each other, Gareth crouched, leaped into their midst, and sent them flying.

"Call the guards!" Ichigo cried. "They are fighting! They will all kill each other!"

"They're only playing," Jason assured him. "It's one of the ways they learn how to be cats. There . . . look at that!" One of the kittens was almost on his hind legs, his paws batting the air in front of Gareth. He sprang, Gareth ducked, seized the kitten, and the two rolled over and over. "That was a good catch! See, now the little one's using his hind legs much better."

The sham battle ended as quickly as it had begun. All

the cats, including Gareth, suddenly stopped, sat on their haunches, and began to wash.

"Yes, I understand," Ichigo said. "They are learning. If only emperors could learn the same way." He sighed. "Of course, when you have an Uncle Fujiwara, I don't suppose it's necessary."

That evening, Ichigo pleaded so hard to take the kittens to his own chambers that Jason at last agreed. Surely nothing could happen to them in the Imperial Palace, Jason thought. But in the morning, when he and Gareth went to the throne room for the kittens' daily game, the boy's jaw dropped. Every kitten was dressed in a tiny embroidered kimono.

"The Imperial Tailors worked all night," Ichigo said proudly.

"But cats don't wear kimonos!"

"My cats shall!"

"But Ichigo," Jason began, "as Master of Imperial Cats . . ."

"No, no, no! I don't care about that. I'm tired of being told what to do. These are my cats. They shall wear what is proper for cats of an emperor!"

"An emperor's cat's no different from any other," Jason began.

But Ichigo folded his arms, turned his head away, and refused to hear any more.

Jason strode angrily out of the throne room, completely forgetting to bump his head on the floor.

Later, when he and Gareth were alone, Jason still felt vexed. "I've never seen anything so ridiculous," he snapped.

"At least Ichigo's showing a little spirit," Gareth said, "even if he's going about it in the wrong way. He really wants to take care of the kittens; he just doesn't know how."

"We'll have to make him get rid of those silly kimonos," Jason said. "That's the first thing."

"No," Gareth said. "That will come in time. The first thing isn't getting them out of the kimonos, it's getting them out of the palace. For a little while at least. You can't have a cat cooped up indoors all the time. There's smells to smell, mice to chase, and so many things that have to be looked at and studied very, very carefully. It's all part of being a cat."

That night, while everyone else in the palace slept, Jason waited alone behind the screens of his chamber. In a few moments Gareth appeared outside. The kittens were with him.

"Come on," Gareth called. "We'll be back before Ichigo wakes up."

Jason slid open a screen and stepped out into the cool garden. With Gareth leading, they crossed the palace grounds. Avoiding the guards at the gate, they passed through the orchard of cherry trees and headed for the center of Kyoto. Behind them, still wearing the Imperial kimonos, padded the five kittens.

9.
Secret Journeys

In Kyoto, Gareth avoided the crowded streets, the tea houses where gaily colored lanterns glowed, the cook shops, the busy inns. Without seeming to think about which direction to take, the black cat found his way easily to the quieter sections and humbler quarters of the city. Through the narrow alleyways, the kittens never lagged behind. Five pairs of eyes, as bright as tiny lanterns, followed Gareth at every turn.

Every so often, Gareth would stop and allow the kittens time to investigate the neighborhood. Whiskers alert, the little ones sniffed the air, dipped their paws into puddles of water, climbed to the tops of bamboo railings, pounced at shadows. They balanced on the rims of rain barrels, then jumped, like divers, back to the ground.

"The kittens won't find any of this in the palace," Gareth said. "Oh, they'll learn a lot there, too; but a cat likes to know what's on both sides of a wall."

"I hope Ichigo doesn't mind," Jason said. "Or Uncle Fujiwara; that would be worse."

"We'll worry about that later," Gareth said. "A cat can always think of something when the time comes. Right now, I'd like to have a look in some of those houses."

Since all of the houses in the quarter were made of paper screens, and rather flimsy ones, Gareth had no trouble finding a way in.

The first house they visited belonged to a carpenter. The workshop, filled with tools and planks of wood, stacks of bamboo, and unfinished pieces of furniture had the sharp, warm scent of wood shavings and sawdust. Gareth, his head raised quizzically, detected something else.

"Rats," he said. He crouched, his muscles tensed; his tail lashed back and forth. "Plenty of them, probably as big as the kittens. They're wicked fighters. Even a grown cat has to watch his step with them. Well, this is as good a place as any for the kittens to learn. Stay here," he warned Jason. "We can move faster if nobody's in the way."

Gareth, with the kittens trotting silently behind, moved through the workshop and disappeared into the shadows.

Jason tiptoed outside and sat, well out of sight, around the corner from the carpenter's house. What a difference, he thought, between the palace and this part of the city. Here, the houses were so jammed together that the whole neighborhood would easily fit into Ichigo's throne room.

No sound came from the workshop. After half an hour, the anxious Jason decided he had better go and find the hunters. But Gareth and the kittens popped out just at that moment.

"That carpenter's going to be grateful in the morning," said Gareth, as he led the procession back to the palace. "We couldn't catch all the rats, but the ones that got away had such a scare that I don't think they'll be back for a while. The kittens did very well. Ichigo should be proud of them."

There was an expedition every night for the rest of the week. Jason always went along to help Gareth keep an eye on the kittens—not that they really needed it. In the course of the week, Jason saw that they had not only grown bigger in size but their walk was more confident and they carried their tails more jauntily.

The kittens still had a lot to learn. During one expedition, a kitten accidentally knocked over some cooking pots. They made such a clatter that the owner of the house woke up. Top-knot bobbing, a broom of twigs in his hand, the man dashed into the room and began shouting fearfully. Jason, Gareth, and the kittens took to their heels and didn't stop until they reached the palace again.

In the throne room next day Uncle Fujiwara paced back and forth, scowling more than usual. "There are strange happenings in Kyoto," the Regent said. "Only this morning a carver of jade reports that his house was invaded by a hundred spirits. He valiantly seized a broom to fight them off, but they disappeared through a hole in the wall."

Jason smiled to himself. Wherever Gareth had taken him, it seemed that people enjoyed exaggerating. How the jade carver could make a hundred spirits out of five kittens Jason could not imagine. But Uncle Fujiwara—and Ichigo, too—never thought of doubting the story.

"And there is more," the Regent went on. "In certain quarters rats have been disappearing from the houses."

"But that's good, isn't it?" Jason asked.

"Speak when you are spoken to, Master of Imperial

Cats," the Regent said angrily. He continued. "Mysterious forces are at work. Seventy-two scholars are now studying this problem. So far, they will only say that none of this took place until the arrival of these foreigners." The Regent gestured contemptuously at Jason and Gareth.

"But I like these foreigners," Ichigo put in.

"You, too; speak when you are spoken to," snapped Uncle Fujiwara. "This is a warning. If this boy and his strange animal have anything to do with it, they will suffer the consequences."

"I don't understand," said Jason, when he and Gareth were alone in their chamber. "You'd think Fujiwara would be glad the rats were disappearing."

"That's another thing about emperors—and regents," Gareth said. "They aren't very fond of changes, even if the changes are for the better."

"Do you think we should take the kittens out again?"

"We can't interrupt their education just because Uncle Fujiwara is in a bad temper," Gareth said. "Don't worry about it. There won't be any trouble."

That night, however, Gareth was wrong. They had stayed out later than usual and dawn had begun to break. At one street corner Jason saw a company of Imperial Guards.

"Just slide along this wall," Gareth whispered. "Very quietly. They'll never notice us."

It would have worked—except for one kitten who lagged behind and, afraid of being separated from the others, began mewing so loudly that the Honorable Imperial Captain turned around. Next moment, Jason, Gareth, and the kittens were surrounded. Recognizing the Imperial Crest on the kimonos, the Honorable Imperial Captain marched everyone back to the palace.

In the throne room, as soon as Ichigo saw them, he leaped to his feet. "How dare you steal the Imperial Kittens!" he cried.

Jason tried to explain what he and Gareth had been doing. Ichigo paid no attention. He fondled the kittens, examined each one for damages, brushed specks of dust from the kimonos. "You are no longer my friend," said Ichigo, almost in tears. "I shall call Uncle Fujiwara and let him decide what to do with you."

"Why don't you make up your own mind for a change," Jason said. "If you think I should have my head chopped off, you don't need to ask your Uncle. Only do one thing. Bring in one of the people we visited; bring in the carpenter, or anybody, and talk to them first."

"You think the words of a carpenter can make any difference?" asked Ichigo.

"I think they'll make a lot of difference," Jason said.

Ichigo finally agreed.

Jason described the quarter they had visited the first night. The Honorable Imperial Captain of Guards recognized it and sent two men to fetch the carpenter.

While they waited, Ichigo sat glumly. The kittens played in front of him, but the Emperor was too preoccupied to notice. Finally, the carpenter was brought in, trembling with fear, convinced that his head would be chopped off at any moment.

"Do you have rats in your house?" Jason asked.

"No, no," the carpenter answered. "Only a week ago this humble and insignificant person was plagued with honorable rats. Now, suddenly, the rats are gone. It is a great miracle. Every day this wretched one gives thanks to the spirits of his ancestors."

"Here are the ones you should thank." Jason pointed to the kittens.

The carpenter dropped to his knees and bumped his head six or eight times against the floor. "Are these the kindly spirits who protected my unworthy home? Blessings, blessings . . ."

"These are cats," Jason said.

"Whatever they may be," said the carpenter, "they have great powers. My wife blesses them; the food for my children is no longer stolen."

The carpenter bowed so much and knocked his head so gratefully that the guards had to carry him out of the throne room and let him recover in the hall.

"He did seem pleased," Ichigo said.

"I know you're an emperor and a Celestial Presence and all that," Jason said, "but if you were anybody else, I'd say you were being selfish. There's no reason why the kittens shouldn't help your people. They certainly aren't doing much good locked up in the palace. Cats aren't toys, just to be played with."

"I know what I'll do," Ichigo said. "I'll have the artists come and paint more pictures. Then, everybody in Japan shall have one."

"That won't do any good."

"But they are most excellent and honorable artists," Ichigo protested.

"It doesn't matter," Jason said. "A *picture* of a cat won't work. You have to have real ones."

Ichigo thought for a moment, then he shook his head. "I don't know what else to do. I shall ask Uncle Fujiwara."

"Can't you forget Uncle Fujiwara?" Jason cried impatiently. "It's time you stopped acting like a baby and started behaving like an emperor!"

Before Jason could finish, Uncle Fujiwara himself appeared in the throne room. "What is that fainting carpenter doing out there?" he shouted. "He's babbling about miracles and spirits with long tails. So!" The Regent caught sight of Jason. "I knew this foreigner had something to do with it!"

"That is true," said Ichigo. "This foreigner has taught me many things about cats—and other matters. I have thought carefully and this is my decision: these kittens are too valuable to remain uselessly in the palace. They shall come and go as they please.

"That's not all," Ichigo added. "When the merchant Sun-Cheng visits us again, he shall be asked to bring more kittens. Enough for every house in Japan!"

"I have heard enough," Uncle Fujiwara said. "You, my worthy nephew, have gone completely mad. It is the influence of this boy. I think it is necessary to dispose of him. And his cat. And these kittens."

Uncle Fujiwara pulled out his sword and seized Jason by the hair. "We will start with this one!"

He threw Jason to the floor and stood over him, sword upraised.

"Stop! I command you!"

Jason had never heard Ichigo use that tone of voice before. Uncle Fujiwara was so surprised that his arm froze motionless in the air.

"This is my Master of Imperial Cats," Ichigo said. "He is under my protection. I order you not to harm him."

Uncle Fujiwara slowly turned and looked curiously at Ichigo. "What did you say?" he asked in a cold voice.

"I order you," Ichigo repeated.

The Regent drew closer to the throne. "Worthy nephew," he said through clenched teeth, "as your adviser and instructor I caution you on your use of words. If there is any ordering to be done here . . ."

"If there is ordering to be done," Ichigo cried, "then I shall do it! I am Emperor, not you!"

"Why you ridiculous, insignificant little . . ." Uncle Fujiwara raised his sword again.

"You threaten me?" Ichigo said. "You dare to threaten your Emperor? I could have you boiled in oil! Humble yourself in the Celestial Presence!"

Ichigo's eyes blazed. For a moment, Jason feared that Uncle Fujiwara would run the boy through. The glances of the Regent and the Emperor locked.

"Your Emperor commands you!"

Jason had never seen such a look of fury as the one that darkened the Regent's face. But Fujiwara was the first to turn his eyes away. He dropped his weapon to the floor and bowed deeply.

Jason and Gareth walked silently from the room.

Near the throne, the kittens played happily with the tassels of Fujiwara's sword.

Italy

.

10.
Odranoel

Ichigo's throne room became a mountainside. Jason looked about for Gareth. Ears cupped forward, whiskers quivering, the cat was crouching at the mouth of a cave, listening. Jason himself heard only a thin breeze that wound a ribbon through the rocks. Below, in the gold and blue of the late afternoon, the mountain fell away into small hills rolling toward the valley. A castle tower rose in the distance, behind a white village and silver-green orchards of olive trees.

"Something's in there," Gareth said. "I can hear it scuffling around." The cat sprang lightly to one of the rocks. "Stay high," he cautioned. "If you don't know what you're going to meet, at least keep on top of it."

Jason followed the cat to the upper arch of the cave and pressed himself against the rocks.

Whatever it was began coming out.

Whatever it was was a boy, lanky, bony, with a shock of bright copper-colored hair. He was a few years older than Jason and much taller. At the cave mouth the boy blinked at the sunlight and blew out the small torch he carried.

Jason, expecting he didn't know what, breathed a sigh of relief. The boy heard, spun quickly, shouted in surprise. His movement started Jason off the rocks; Gareth bushed out his fur. For a moment everybody looked terrified of everybody else—Gareth bristling, Jason scrambling up from the pebbles, the boy raising his torch like a sword. Then the boy began to laugh.

"That was wonderful," he chuckled. "At first I thought you were a bear. And look at your cat! His fur's still up. He must have expected a monster to come and carry him off."

"He didn't expect anything of the kind," said Jason. "He does that when he's surprised. He doesn't like to be made fun of, either," Jason added.

"I'm not making fun," said the boy. "I think it was beautiful. Did you see his eyes? They were like round fires. And the way he had his paws, all stiff in front of him, with the claws ready. And his jaws open; you could see his teeth."

"Didn't you ever see a cat before?"

"Of course I did," said the boy. "Hundreds of them. But just because you've seen something, it doesn't mean you stop looking. There's always something you didn't see before."

The tall boy, whose name was Leonardo, led the way down the mountain path. They skirted the village and the olive trees. Hatless, Leonardo strode with his head high and thrown back a little; the bright hair made his face look as if the sun were shining on it. He talked rapidly about a dozen different things, one after the other, without waiting for Jason to answer. About volcanoes. Had Jason ever seen any? What made fire come out of the ground? Was there a place inside the earth that still burned? If so, why wasn't the ground hot? Leonardo's voice was strange, excited, and made Jason think of bright colors, all shifting back and forth.

By the time they reached the rambling farmhouse with its flower gardens and vegetable gardens, the vineyards heavy with misted clusters of grapes, Leonardo's conversation had turned from volcanoes to fish to beetles to birds.

Inside the house, Leonardo's family already sat at the long dinner table. A man in a handsomely tailored doublet looked up irritably. "If you're late again, you can find your own dinner in the woods!"

The older man beside him chuckled. "I think it will be a long day, Piero, when you keep Leonardo from the table —no matter how late he is." He turned to the copper-haired boy. "So, what have you found this time? Beetles? Butterflies?"

"A boy and a cat," Leonardo said.

Everyone noticed Jason and Gareth and began talking all at once. Ser Piero, Leonardo's father, pounded the table for silence. He called Jason over and looked at him carefully. "Now, speak up, boy! Give me the truth. You're a runaway apprentice, I can guess that much. What's your trade? Mason? Clothmaker? Who's your master? What is his guild?"

"Food before questions," said the older man, with a wink at Jason. He was, as Jason learned, Leonardo's uncle, Ser Francesco.

"At least let him stay a while," Leonardo said.

Ser Piero grumbled, but gestured Jason to a seat at the

table. Gareth curled at the boy's feet. Leonardo's mother (his stepmother, Jason discovered later), a frail woman with a pale, kindly face, called a servant for extra plates.

Ser Piero was still annoyed. "Leonardo must learn to be punctual," he said to Francesco. "All this wandering around, climbing mountains, finding stray cats and runaway apprentices. . . . You tell me, Francesco. Is this a discipline for the mind? A notary must have discipline."

"There is time, time," Ser Francesco said.

"Time!" cried Piero. "None at all! He is half-grown already. No, no. He must come to Florence and begin his work. Every Vinci has been a notary."

A knock at the door interrupted Ser Piero. In came a heavy-shouldered, red-faced man—a farmer, Jason judged —carrying a flat piece of wood.

"Ah, Jacopo." Ser Piero turned. "What brings you here?"

The farmer doffed his round cap and made a quick bow to the family. "I would ask a favor, Ser Piero," he said. "Not for myself, for my wife. You know the ideas women get." He held out the piece of wood. "She has decided now that we must have a picture for our bedchamber. I had cut this board from one of my fig trees—you know, the one the storm blew down—and nothing will satisfy her but an artist must paint something on it."

Ser Piero took the board and turned it around in his hands. "It is a little crooked," he said. "The surface is none too good. What would you have me do with it? The Vincis are notaries, not painters."

"As a favor," Jacopo said, "take it with you when you go to the city again. There must be a painter in Florence who will decorate it cheaply. A few ducats are all I can afford."

Ser Piero nodded. "Very well, Jacopo. I shall attend to it."

Jacopo bowed again. "I thank you, Ser Piero. I hate to trouble you. But it is for my wife, you understand."

After the farmer had left the house, Leonardo picked up the board and examined it carefully. "Why take it to Florence, father?" he asked. "I can decorate it here."

Ser Piero gave a loud laugh. "Francesco, do you hear the boy? He can decorate it!" He turned to his son. "My dear Leonardo, Jacopo wants a painting for his ducats. A real painting by a real artist."

"I can draw," said Leonardo, "and I can make my own colors."

Piero sniffed. "Ser Leonardo talks like a master craftsman."

"Hold on, Piero," Ser Francesco put in. "I have seen the boy's sketches. They are not without skill."

"I don't deny," Ser Piero said, "that he has a little knack, for a boy his age. But they are trifles, the work of idle hands and an idle mind. He should be thinking about business, not about daubing paint."

"Why not?" Francesco asked. "If he prefers it? Art is an honest trade."

"As an amusement," Ser Piero said, "it is harmless. But to do nothing else, no. For a notary, it is not suitable."

"But I'm not a notary," Leonardo cried.

"You will be," Ser Piero answered sharply. "As soon as I can arrange it. I can see I have already waited too long."

Leonardo tightened his lips and turned away angrily.

"Now then, now then," Ser Francesco said. "There should be no quarreling between father and son. As an honest man, Piero, you must know there is only one fair answer to this."

"I do," said Piero. "He must come to business immediately."

"Let the boy have his chance," Francesco urged. "He wants to paint Jacopo's board? Let him. Then take it to Florence. Show it to Ser Andrea Verrocchio, a friend of mine. Ser Andrea is a master of all the arts. He will give you his opinion."

Ser Piero hesitated. "And suppose Leonardo ruins the board?"

"I will buy another to replace it," said Francesco, "and pay for it out of my own purse."

Ser Piero thought for a few moments. "Very well," he said. "It is time we decide the question once and for all." He tapped a forefinger on the board in Leonardo's hands. "You think yourself an artist? We shall see what you do with this."

Clutching the board, Leonardo jumped to his feet. "Yes," he cried. "We shall see! Come on!" He beckoned to Jason. The two boys, followed by Gareth, hurried upstairs to Leonardo's room.

Tacked on the door was a sheet of paper with a strange inscription Jason could not read at all.

"It says 'Keep Out, No Visitors,'" Leonardo explained.

"It doesn't look like it," said Jason.

"That's because I wrote it backwards," Leonardo said. "Don't you ever look at things backwards? *Odranoel!* That's my name, spelled the other way around. That's what I did on the sign, but double backwards. If you hold it up to a mirror, the letters come right again. It's my secret code."

"But if you don't want anybody in your room," Jason said, "I don't see why you wrote a notice nobody can read."

"Nobody pays any attention to signs," said Leonardo. "The notice is just there to be mysterious. If I want to keep people out, I *tell* them so."

Inside, Jason looked with amazement—tables crowded with piles of paper; collections of butterflies, rocks, pressed flowers. A squirrel raced back and forth in a small cage. In another cage, a sleepy green snake lay coiled. Great bottles and jars held clumps of moss and long-tailed, speckled lizards. From another bottle, a few fish stared at the inquisitive Gareth.

On a table, Leonardo had set a water bottle over a candle flame. "Did you ever notice how the bubbles come up?" Leonardo asked. "I've been watching them. There must be something inside, something invisible—I don't know what it is. Perhaps the philosophers in Florence know and someday I'll ask them. First, I want to try to find out for myself."

Leonardo reached down and took a sheaf of papers from a pile on the floor. He handed them to Jason. "This is what my father was arguing about."

Jason leafed through them. There were drawings of plants and animals, a picture of the squirrel in its cage; on one sheet, Leonardo had sketched a flower, very large, and cut down the middle to show the inside. Ser Piero's face, sober and serious, looking exactly like him, covered another page; and on another, a cartoon of Ser Francesco in the middle of a sneeze.

"What will you paint for Jacopo?" asked Jason.

"I don't know yet," Leonardo said. "I have to look at this board for a while. It is badly bent, at that. I'll have to smooth it down."

The boy pushed aside the papers and cleared a space on the table. He arranged the board, pulled over a candle, and sat down. The candlelight on Leonardo's coppery hair reflected in the boy's face as a golden haze. He frowned, bit his lip, and squinted at the board first from one angle then another.

"What are you going to do now?" asked Jason.

Leonardo did not answer. Nor did he answer when Jason repeated the question. The boy seemed to have forgotten completely that anyone else was in the room. There was, Jason saw, no use in talking to him any more. Leonardo's attention was on the work in front of him and nowhere else.

Jason closed the door quietly as he left the room. He and Gareth found their way down the hall to the room Leonardo's mother had prepared.

"I've never met anyone like that," Jason said. "I've never known anybody who watched everything so much."

"Cats do it," Gareth said. "You'd be surprised how much a cat can learn just by watching."

From Leonardo's room came a muffled explosion and the tinkle of glass.

"That must be the water bottle," Gareth said. "I was afraid that would happen if he kept on boiling it."

Jason expected to hear everyone in the house running to Leonardo's room. But there were no further sounds. The Vinci family, Jason decided, must be used to explosions.

11.
Ser Piero Sees a Picture

When Jason and Gareth climbed out of bed, Leonardo was already awake—or else he hadn't slept at all. Jason found him still sitting at his table. The lights had all gone out of his face, and in the early morning he merely looked like a sleepy boy who has stayed up most of the night and needs a haircut.

The squirrel exercised frantically in its cage. Gareth jumped up and pressed his nose to the bars, studying the little animal racing as fast as it could, spinning its wheel and always staying in the same place.

"Have you decided what to paint?" Jason asked.

Leonardo only grunted. He tossed over Jacopo's board.

"You straightened it!" Jason said. "And it's all smooth and white." He examined the board. Leonardo must have spent hours working on the surface. It would be perfect for painting.

"But there's nothing on it," Leonardo sighed. "First, there were so many things I wanted to paint I couldn't decide which to do. Then, they all flew out of my head and I couldn't think of anything. I wanted to do something—I don't know—different. Now there's nothing," he added glumly. "All the pictures are gone."

"You'll find something," Jason said. "There's no hurry."

"I want to do it now," Leonardo said with irritation. "My father's gone to Florence. He'll be back tomorrow or the next day. I want it ready for him."

The squirrel had stopped its racing. Chattering and scolding, it jumped at Gareth. Surprised, the cat bristled and pulled back.

"That's what I want!" Leonardo cried, snapping his fingers. "That's my picture! I should have thought of it before. Yes, yes," he went on excitedly, "a picture of a cat. They're the most beautiful animals in the world—and the hardest to paint, if you really want the picture to look like a cat.

"Remember yesterday, when we all scared each other up in the mountains? He looked the same way then. That's the idea I want."

"Are you going to paint the cave, too?" Jason asked. "And me hanging on the rocks?"

"Of course not," Leonardo said impatiently. "I'm just going to paint your cat."

"But I thought you said . . ."

"I said that's the *idea* I want," Leonardo explained. "It doesn't mean you have to show everything else. The cat's the main thing. But when somebody looks at the painting, it should make them think of all the rest. They should look at it and say, 'Now, here's a cat; he's angry and frightened and ready to fight, something must have scared him.' Then they'll wonder what it was.

"Maybe they won't use those words," Leonardo went on, "but if it's any good, a painting should make you think about a lot of other things. In a painting there's always more than what you see. . . . " Leonardo stopped and frowned. "He doesn't look bristly any more. Make him do it again."

"I can't make him," Jason said. "He only does it when he feels like it."

"I could think up something to scare him," Leonardo suggested. "Nothing serious. Just enough to . . ."

"Oh no you won't," Jason said. As much as he liked this strange, copper-haired boy, he had no intention of letting him annoy Gareth. "You can paint his picture all you want, if he's sitting down or sleeping or walking around, but no more than that."

Leonardo looked disappointed. "I suppose I can remember how he looked when he was angry," he said at last. "You know, that might even be better. Because I can change a lot of things; it doesn't have to look exactly like him. Yes, that's what I'll do."

The boy picked up a bit of charcoal and began sketching rapidly on the back of an old sheet of paper. "The thing about cats," Leonardo said, working along until the paper was covered, "is the way they're made. Those muscles in the back legs. Can you imagine how strong they must be? That's why cats can jump so high. And the back, it can move almost any way, like a sword blade.

"Everything is in balance," Leonardo went on, "all the muscles and bones and joints. That's what I want in the painting, too."

"Well, I hope you aren't going to paint bones and muscles," Jason said. "I don't think anybody would like that at all."

"Of course I'm not going to paint just bones and muscles," Leonardo said. "But *I* know where they are, even if nobody else sees them. And that's bound to make the picture better."

Jason shook his head. "I don't see how you ever learned all this."

"My Uncle Francesco told me a lot," Leonardo said. "The rest I figured out for myself. It's easy when you stop to think—and watch."

Leonardo crumpled his sketch paper and threw it on the floor. He picked up the board and looked lovingly at the untouched surface. Jason could guess that the boy would soon forget everything else. He was right. In a minute or two, Leonardo was lost in his work. Jason was tempted to look over his shoulder, but, rather than disturb Leonardo, he picked up Gareth and went downstairs.

All that day and all that evening Leonardo stayed locked in his room. On the way to bed Jason noticed a new and bigger sign added to the other one on Leonardo's door. It said "POSITIVELY KEEP OUT" and was written the right way except for the signature "ODRANOEL." Leonardo's mother had left a tray of food at the door, but it was untouched.

"I hope he's all right in there," said Jason. "I wonder if we should go in and see."

"Cats don't go butting in on each other," Gareth said, "unless they're looking for a fight. If you bother Leonardo now, that's just what you might get. Don't worry, he'll come out when he's ready."

The following morning Leonardo's door stood open.

Jason peeked in and saw the copper-haired boy hunched over the table, his tousled head cradled in his arms. Jason was about to leave again, but Leonardo stirred and straightened up. He gave Jason a pale smile.

"It's done," he said.

Jason hurried into the room. "Where? May I see it?"

"No, no, no!" Leonardo jumped up and ran to the chair he had been using for an easel. A paint-soiled cloth covered the board. The copper-haired boy stood in front of it. "I don't want anybody to see it yet. Not until my father comes home."

"How did it turn out?" asked Jason.

Leonardo had a curious half-smile. He did not answer.

When his father and uncle returned to the farm at dusk, Leonardo asked them to come to his room. Jason was surprised, knowing his friend to be fussy about visitors; but when he entered the room he saw that Leonardo had arranged the painting, still covered, near the window, where it caught the last rays of the sun. He had also lit several candles on the table. Leonardo's mother stood in the doorway, watching her son with a look half of pride, half of puzzlement. Ser Piero glanced around the room at the squirrel in its cage, the snake, the bunches of dried leaves, the rocks, as if he wished they weren't there.

"Sit down, please, Father," Leonardo said.

Ser Piero shrugged. "This must be a special event."

"I've been working on a picture for Jacopo," Leonardo began; then he talked about the board, how he had steamed it straight—all in such great detail that Ser Piero shifted his feet restlessly.

Jason saw Piero hide a yawn in the palm of his hand and wondered why Leonardo simply didn't pull away the cloth and have done with it. A moment later Jason noticed Leonardo's hand reach for a length of cord. By this time Ser Piero's attention had wandered so far that he did not realize the cloth was gradually being raised from the painting. Leonardo kept on talking. Ser Piero fidgeted.

"Father, look!" Leonardo said abruptly.

Ser Piero turned, blinked—and leaped straight up. With a roar of terror he knocked over his chair. The rock collection sprayed across the floor; the servant girl screamed. "Watch out! It's ready to jump!" shouted Ser Piero. "Out! Out! Everybody!"

If Jason hadn't suspected something, he would have run for his life. Even at that, even knowing it was only a painting, he felt the hairs rise on his neck. Gareth crouched and growled. Leonardo had drawn a cat, but not exactly a cat. He had worked from his memory of Gareth, bristling and angry, but he had changed many things. The eyes in the painting were Gareth's blazing orange eyes; the rest was part cat and part—Jason didn't know what. But the animal looked real enough to spring from the board and tear the room apart with its ferocious claws. It was the most perfect painting Jason had ever seen—and the most frightening.

Ser Francesco was the first to realize it was only a picture and began to laugh at the top of his voice. "Oh, Piero, Piero, you have been well surprised!"

Piero, whose face was still as pale as paste, frowned angrily.

Francesco clapped him on the shoulder. "Confess,

now! You never expected anything like it. You didn't think Leonardo could do it. Admit it! Fair is fair!"

Leonardo's mother came forward and raised her voice for the first time. "Piero," she said calmly, "this is not the work of a notary. This is the work of an artist. I have listened to you and Leonardo argue back and forth, and I have said nothing. I knew that what you decided would be right and I did not want to interfere. But I tell you now, Piero, that if you force Leonardo to be a notary, you will be wrong."

Piero said nothing for a while. He looked at the painting, then back at his son.

"I did not mean to force the boy into anything," he said. "Ideas change when you are young. I did not believe he was really serious. True, I wanted him to be a notary, but only yesterday I spoke with the artist, Ser Andrea. I had planned to take whatever Leonardo painted and show it to him.

"I no longer need Ser Andrea's judgment," Piero said. "I have eyes to see for myself. He will study painting in Florence. And he will start now."

"Bravo!" cried Francesco. "But Leonardo had to scare you out of your wits before you made up your mind."

"Francesco," said Ser Piero, "you can forget about that part of it."

Ser Piero was as good as his word. Next day Uncle Francesco, Leonardo's mother, and the whole Vinci household helped the boy pack for his trip. In the confusion no one noticed when Jason and Gareth slipped away from the farm and made their way across the flowering meadow.

"You know, Gareth," Jason said, "if it hadn't been for

you I don't think Ser Piero would ever have let Leonardo study painting. You were the one who gave him the idea for the picture and, after that, everything worked out."

"No, that's not exactly true," said Gareth. "With a boy like Leonardo, it would have happened one way or another. He didn't need me or anyone else to give him an idea. He would have found it himself. So I can't really say I helped."

"Well," said Jason reluctantly, "if you say so. But I like to think you did."

High against a cloud a lone bird played with the breeze. A butterfly danced and flickered across the meadow. Boy and cat followed its bright wings until it was out of sight.

Peru

.

1555

12.
Don Diego

Instead of a field of flowers, Jason and Gareth stood in a room almost as cluttered as Leonardo's. Here, the clutter was different. Against one of the stone walls leaned a heavy musket; a couple of Spanish-style helmets, with round tops and curved brims, had rolled into a corner, along with a breastplate that needed polishing. Piles of what seemed to be laundry waited to be sent out; there were two left-footed boots, a sword that would have been most warlike had it been sharp. At a wooden table, his head in his arms, the owner of these items snored peacefully. However, as soon as Jason moved, the sleeper started up, blinking; except for the curled mustache and pointed beard, which didn't quite appear to belong to him, the man looked like a surprised fish.

"Who . . . what . . . ," he stammered. Noticing Gareth, the man suddenly began to beam delightedly. "Of course!" he cried. "The cat I ordered! But how did you get here so fast? I gave the letter to a messenger only six weeks ago. This is really amazing. All the way from Peru to Spain and back again." He stopped abruptly. "It is my cat, isn't it? There's no mistake about the delivery? One cat to be sent to Don Diego Francisco Hernández del Gato Herrera y Robles?"

All the while, Don Diego was patting Gareth fondly; and before Jason could answer, the Spaniard picked up Gareth and cradled him in his arms. "No, no," Don Diego said. "There couldn't be a mistake. No, I've waited too long. It must have cost a fortune! But it's worth it. Just to have a cat. Ah, a cat. Even the sound of the name is worth another fortune."

Don Diego wiped a tear from his eye. "Forgive me," he sniffled through his mustache. "But we are an emotional family, on my mother's side. Oh, it's been so lonely here," he added. "I didn't ask to be in the army, but my family, on my father's side, didn't know what else to do with me. And they spent so much money buying me a captain's commission I can't disappoint them."

"Bought you a commission?" Jason asked.

Don Diego looked at him, puzzled. "Naturally," he said. "How else would a gentleman start off in the army? But I didn't think it would turn out like this. I'll tell you one thing," Don Diego looked over his shoulder and dropped his voice to a whisper, "the whole business has gone wrong from the beginning. Pizarro and his friends came looking for gold. Oh, they found it, you can believe that. These Indians have more gold than I've ever seen in my life. Plenty for everybody. The Indians would have given us all we wanted. But no, that wasn't enough for Pizarro and the Conquerors. They started being greedy and quarrelsome—and plotting against each other. To make a long story short, there's not one of them left alive today.

"Now there's nothing but fighting," Don Diego went on sadly. "We fight the Indians; the Indians fight us. And then we fight among ourselves. The Viceroy, sent by His Majesty himself, doesn't know what to do. Well, I don't care. I have my cat; that's all that matters to me. They can keep the gold, much good it may do them. My cat," Don Diego repeated, dreamily.

"I'm glad you like cats," Jason said. "But there's something you don't understand. My cat and I, well, we're together. I mean . . ."

"Of course!" Don Diego cried. "How thoughtful of my family, on my mother's side. To send a cat—and a boy to help me look after it. Yes, that's it. You can be my orderly. Then I won't have to put up with that lazy, impudent Pedro. I try to shout at him, but he won't listen or else he talks back. He refuses to keep my quarters tidy—see for yourself." Don Diego flung out his arms in despair. "I can't seem to keep things straight alone. But now it's all going to be different. A cat! It feels homey already."

A trumpet blared outside. Don Diego clapped a hand to his head. "I'm late for close-order drill. I forgot. All the excitement . . ." He began rushing around the room, stumbling over the laundry, trying to buckle on his breastplate, while the helmet, much too big for his head, slipped down over his eyes.

Jason decided this was no time to mention Don Diego's mistake. He helped the Captain struggle into his armor. With half his buckles flying, the breathless Don Diego picked up his sword and tumbled headlong out the door.

Jason watched the Spaniard fumble his way across the

barracks yard. A company of pike men stiffened to attention. From this distance Jason could not tell what orders Don Diego was shouting, but they must have been wrong, for the soldiers, all as stiff as their own pikes, kept marching off in different directions, wheeling and bumping into one another.

"Well," Jason said, "I've never seen a soldier like *that*."

"Wearing a uniform doesn't make someone a soldier," Gareth said. "I think he'd rather be home."

"He did seem awfully confused about things," Jason said. "I don't know what he'll do when his own cat arrives."

"We'll see about that later," Gareth said. "The only thing a cat worries about is what's happening right now. As we tell the kittens, you can only wash one paw at a time."

Jason did his best to put Don Diego's room in order, but it was hopeless. The Captain had so many odds and ends of things, bits of candles, belts with the buckles missing, rusted pistols, a couple of oil paintings (one portrait from his father's side of the family, one from his mother's) that Jason finally put it all in one heap in a corner of the room. Sheets of parchment covered the table, and when Jason tried to straighten them up he could not avoid noticing what Don Diego had been writing.

"It looks like he's trying to make a dictionary," Jason said to Gareth. "Here's all the Indian words on one side and here's where he explains what they mean.

"He's been writing a lot about the Indians, too," Jason went on. "He calls them Incas. There's pages and pages about how they live and what they wear—I wonder why he's doing that?"

"It might be that he's lonesome and homesick and doesn't have anything else to pass the time," said Gareth, who had curled up in Don Diego's spare helmet. "Or he may just be the kind of man who's very interested in what's happening, what he sees and does, and wants to make sure he'll remember."

Jason glanced through the papers. "I think he'd be better off writing history than trying to be a soldier."

"I'm sure he'd agree with you," Gareth said. "But, I suppose his family thought he belonged in the army."

"I guess they did," Jason said, "at least, on his father's side."

Toward the middle of the afternoon, Don Diego—flushed, smiling, his helmet all crooked—burst into the room. From the officers' mess he had brought food for dinner. Humming happily, he set it down on the table.

"Now," said Don Diego, rubbing his hands, "something to eat, then a nap, and after that—some tricks."

"You're going to do tricks?" Jason asked eagerly.

"Me? Goodness, no! The cat will."

"The cat?" Jason asked, perplexed. "But he doesn't do tricks."

"Perhaps he doesn't now," said Don Diego, raising a finger. "But we'll teach him. I've been looking forward to it all day. Time and patience, that's all it takes. And I have plenty of both."

"Did you ever teach a cat tricks before?" Jason asked.

"No, no, I can't say that I have," Don Diego answered. "But I've always wanted to."

"If you had," Jason went on, "you'd know that cats won't do tricks. Oh, they'll do them, but when *they* feel like it. And they'll make up their own, so it's no use trying to have them learn *your* tricks."

"But they're intelligent . . ."

"That doesn't have anything to do with it," Jason said. "With a cat, it's just not the same. If you wanted a pet to sit up and beg or play dead or give you his paw, you should have asked for a dog. If you wanted a pet to talk, you should have ordered a parrot.

"Some animals are good at some things," Jason explained, "and some are good at others. Cats are good at being cats, and that's enough."

Don Diego's mustache drooped in disappointment. For a moment Jason was afraid the Captain would cry. The Spaniard looked so terribly sad that Jason wished he hadn't said anything.

"I suppose I don't really know anything about cats," Don Diego said glumly. "I've never had one of my own. There was a cat in our family, on my mother's side, and I always admired it, and that's why I wanted one sent to me. I see now it was a mistake—another mistake." He sighed deeply. "I'm always making them."

"It wasn't a mistake at all," Jason said encouragingly. "Cats don't have to do tricks to be fun. Just watching them and playing with them is fun. Try it. You'll see what I mean."

Don Diego said he would try, although he still looked disappointed. After their nap, the Spaniard made no attempt to teach Gareth tricks. Instead, Don Diego sat down at his table and began working with his papers.

"I learned something new today," he said, brightening a little. "Did you know that Inca mothers stand their children up in holes in the ground so they won't run away? The children, that is? Isn't that amazing?" With his quill pen moving furiously, Don Diego made a long note of it.

Gareth had hopped up on Don Diego's table, where he sat watching the quill. Each time Don Diego came to the end of a line Gareth hooked out a padded paw and caught at the pen. The Captain looked up in surprise, then began to chuckle. "Now, that is a kind of trick, isn't it," he said. "It's a game he thought up by himself, so it's really better than a trick!"

Later, Gareth stretched out, purring, on the table. Don Diego leaned back and stroked the cat's ears. "You know," he said to Jason, "this cat makes me feel very pleasant. Isn't that strange? Just sitting here with him—I don't know —everything seems cozier. I don't think I'd like it if he sat up and begged. It wouldn't be . . . dignified, somehow. Maybe you're right, after all.

"Like me being a soldier," Don Diego added, sadly. "It's as silly as trying to teach a cat to do tricks."

In the days that followed, Don Diego was perfectly happy to have Gareth behave just like any cat; and he admitted, finally, that it was more fun that way. While Don Diego drilled his soldiers, Jason gradually put the room in order. After that, there was little for him and Gareth to do in the barracks. During the afternoons, they walked through the city and into the valley.

The name of the city was Cuzco, and the Incas had built it long before the Spaniards had arrived. The houses were mainly of stone; the streets very straight and well kept. In a way it reminded Jason of Egypt with its walls and palaces; there was even a great stone pyramid higher up on the mountain.

Of the Incas, Jason saw nothing. Since the Spaniards had captured Cuzco, the Inca warriors had withdrawn to the valley. There were a few Indians in the fields, but these were of the tribes the Incas themselves had conquered. As Don Diego explained it, the Incas were the rulers of all the other Indians in Peru. Now these rulers were fighting for their lives.

"I wish I could see a real Inca," Jason said one day, when he and Gareth had wandered a little beyond the city. To Jason's surprise, the cat did not answer. Then Jason understood why. In the field, as if they had risen from nowhere, stood four warriors in capes and striped leggings. Jason snatched Gareth up and tried to run.

One of the warriors whirled a three-stranded rope with heavy metal balls at the ends. An instant later, Jason and Gareth lay on the ground, tangled in the weighted cords. Lances leveled, the Incas moved forward.

13.
Sayri Tupac

The Incas had a small camp and village at the edge of the valley. Still trussed up like flies in a spiderweb, Jason and Gareth clung to each other while the warriors carried them into the camp and dumped them in front of Sayri Tupac, the Great Inca himself.

Jason had never seen a man so brilliantly dressed. Over a long tunic the Inca wore a brightly decorated cape; around his forehead were colored braids, with tassels and bits of gold. From his ears hung enormous disks of pure gold. The Inca turned a handsome, bronzed face toward Jason—a face that was severe, commanding, and at the same time filled with a deep sadness.

"Our enemies lie at our feet," Sayri Tupac said. "Just as my father and my brothers have lain at the feet of the Conquerors. The Spaniards have asked for much gold to ransom my brothers. Now the Inca shall demand the gold back again as a ransom for you.

"We have paid," the Inca went on. "We shall see if the Conquerors will do as much. If not . . . there shall be two heads on our battle standards. A message has already been sent to Cuzco," he said. "Your lives depend on the answer."

Jason and Gareth were made to sit against the outside wall of an earthen hut. The Great Inca had nothing further to say to them, but a few of the warriors and some of the women and children of the village gathered to peer curiously not at Jason, but at Gareth. The Incas had seen boys before, in the Spanish garrison. Jason guessed there were no cats in Peru, for he heard one of the men explain that the animal must be some new kind of black puma.

Jason tried not to think of Sayri Tupac's words. If the Spaniards were busy fighting each other, Jason doubted they would take time to think about a boy and a cat. Certainly, they wouldn't give up any of the gold. Sayri Tupac's remarks about two heads on the battle standards did not make Jason feel very cheerful. But, as Gareth had said, you can only wash one paw at a time. To keep his mind off what might happen Jason tried to interest himself in the activity around him.

The more he watched them, the more the Incas reminded him of the Egyptians. Although their costumes were different, the Incas had the same dignity and graceful movements. In addition, the flashing gold of the Inca warriors' earrings, the feathered headdresses, the glittering lances gave the humble camp village the look of an imperial court. Jason could easily imagine how splendid the Incas had been in their great palaces at Cuzco. Like the Egyptians, the Incas had their own scribes—for the wool-robed men busy counting the stocks of provisions were surely scribes, Jason thought. Instead of clay tablets, the Incas seemed to keep their records on long cords made up of many strands of colored, knotted strings.

A few llamas, tended by a young herd boy, wandered past. These animals looked like very large sheep or very small, woolly camels, and they, too, had a quiet dignity about them. They gave Jason and Gareth a solemn glance, then ambled on.

The cords were putting Jason's legs to sleep. He tried to follow Gareth's example by relaxing and drowsing a little. He had just managed to close his eyes and rest when a great shout went up from the warriors. Jason twisted around as far as the cords allowed. At the far end of the village he saw the figure of a man on horseback. It was Don Diego.

The Spaniard reined up near the platform on which Sayri Tupac had his throne. Dismounting, the Spaniard caught his foot in the stirrup and nearly went flat on his face. Poor Don Diego looked terrified and uncomfortable. His helmet was crooked and, with no one to help him, his armor was on all wrong. Jason's heart sank. As much as he liked Don Diego, the awkward Spaniard hardly looked like the man to bargain with the glorious, stately Sayri Tupac.

Don Diego approached the throne. He began to speak, but his helmet slipped down over one ear. With a gesture of impatience, Don Diego pullled off his headpiece and threw it on the ground. He unbuckled his armor, too, and let it drop from his body like a shell.

"There," said Don Diego, "that's a lot better."

Jason could not believe his eyes. Without the heavy armor, dressed only in a simple doublet, Don Diego seemed taller and straighter. He held his head proudly and, when he spoke, his voice rang clearly and calmly.

"I do not wear the armor of the Conquerors," Don Diego said. "I greet you as one man to another. Your soldiers have taken two of my friends. I ask you to return them to me."

"Do the Spaniards talk of friendship?" Sayri Tupac asked scornfully. "We offered them friendship. They wanted only our gold."

"I understand your anger," Don Diego said. "But your quarrel is with men, not with a boy and an animal. If you are indeed a man and a warrior, you will understand that. You will let me take their place."

Sayri Tupac turned his eyes away, but he did not answer. "There has been too much killing," Don Diego went on. "The world has changed, for Spaniards and Incas both. Neither of us can undo what has been done. We must learn to live together, not die together."

Don Diego's voice rose over the camp. He spoke now of the Incas themselves. He reminded them of the wise laws they had made, of the mighty temples and palaces they had built. War could do nothing but destroy them. He spoke of their poetry and dances, the history of the ancient tribe. To Jason, it seemed that Don Diego knew more about the Incas than the Incas themselves.

When he finished, it was Sayri Tupac's turn to speak. "I have listened with wonder," the Great Inca said. "No Spaniard before has spoken in words we could understand. If the Conquerors could only see that we want nothing but to go in peace. If they could see us as men, with our own ways . . ."

"I shall try to show them," Don Diego said. "One man can promise nothing, but I shall do my best."

"That is ransom enough," said the Inca. "Understanding is better than gold. Take the boy and the small black puma," he added. "You shall go from here unharmed."

In his barracks room in Cuzco Don Diego spent two days writing at top speed. He hardly took time to eat or sleep, never put on his armor, and paid no attention to the trumpet calls from the square.

"I'm sending a memorandum to the Viceroy," he told Jason. "I think half the trouble is that nobody knows what the Incas are really like. It's time they found out."

Jason could not get over the change in Don Diego. The Spaniard whistled gaily, walked about briskly; even his mustache looked more cheerful. One afternoon, Don Diego burst into the room and brandished a sheet of parchment.

"A message from the Viceroy!" he cried. "He wants me to go to Lima and be his adviser! He says it would be a waste—a waste of time, mind you—to have someone like me drilling soldiers all day!"

The Spaniard did a little dance, fell over his own feet, hugged Jason and Gareth. "No more of this," he crowed, waving a hand at the helmets and breastplates. "No more bugles, no more 'Company, attention!' Now I can just be myself and do what I know how to do!

"There's another note, too," Don Diego said with a frown. "I don't understand. It says a cat has arrived from Spain at the request of Don Diego Francisco Hernández del Gato Herrera y Robles. Now, there's either two of me or my family, on my mother's side, has sent two cats. I must look into that. Meantime, you can start packing."

Don Diego hurried to the door. "I'll be right back," he called. "I want to show the General this letter. Somehow I think he'll be very happy about it."

After the Spaniard had gone, Jason and Gareth looked at each other. "Well," Jason said after a moment, "I never thought Don Diego would end up in the government."

"He'll be good at it," Gareth said. "Trying to make someone do what they aren't really good at is foolish. Don Diego realized that himself. We cats always knew it. How do you think I'd feel if I had to dress up in armor and drill soldiers all day?"

"That's silly," Jason said. "You wouldn't let anybody do that to you in the first place."

"Because I know I'm a cat," Gareth said. "Don Diego's just found out he's a man."

"By the way," Jason asked, "what is Don Diego going to do with *two* cats?"

"He'll only have one," Gareth said. "Because," the cat added with a wink, "we won't have time to wait for him."

The Isle of Man

·

1588

14.
Dulcinea

They were, suddenly, on a narrow beach. Sunlight glinted through the cracks of a gray sky; a salty wind hummed in Jason's ears.

"I hope Don Diego found his own cat all right," Jason said.

"I'm sure he did," Gareth answered. "But look over there. I think we've found something ourselves."

Jason shaded his eyes. A tiny speck bobbed on top of the waves. "I can't tell what it is," Jason said. "A piece of wood—it's too small for a boat."

The tide drew the speck closer. In a few minutes it almost reached the shore. It was half a barrel.

Jason ran splashing through the surf. In the barrel, in a nest of sailcloth, sat a mother cat and a half-a-dozen kittens. "Gareth, come quickly!" Jason called, pulling the barrel to a dry part of the beach.

Gareth trotted over to investigate. The mother cat jumped out and looked at Jason suspiciously. It was only then that Jason realized she had no tail.

"You're safe now," Gareth told her. "My friend and I are traveling together. He knows about the privilege. We're allowed to talk—when we're alone, of course. Under the circumstances, I'm sure you can talk with him, too. That is," Gareth added, "if you'd like."

The mother cat, who was rather portly, plumped herself down on the sand. She breathed heavily and, had she been human, Jason would have expected her to bring out a handkerchief and fan herself. All she kept saying was, "Terrible! Simply terrible!"

Finally, after she had shaken herself and given her coat a few licks, she turned to Jason.

"Believe me," she said, "that's my last sea voyage. The last! You can take my word for it."

"But," asked Jason, "what would a cat be doing at sea?"

"For luck, of course," said the tailless cat, whose name, as Jason learned, was Dulcinea. "All sailors keep cats aboard ship; don't tell me you didn't know that.

"My ship," Dulcinea went on, "was the finest in the Spanish Armada. We were sailing against England, the whole Spanish fleet—that was a sight, let me tell you! Last night a storm came up. I've never seen anything like it in my life. Split us from stem to stern! The first mate packed my kittens and me in a barrel—the best he could do, poor fellow. I don't say it was comfortable, but at least we stayed afloat. No, never again. I'll stay on land."

"I suppose you just used up all your luck," Jason said.

"My dear boy," answered Dulcinea, "it's not *my* fault the storm came up. Or that the ship was wrecked. Luck is one thing; seamanship is another. I simply cannot be held responsible."

"I hope your kittens are all right," Jason said, realizing he had been tactless.

"Poor things," said Dulcinea. "They had the fright of their lives." She picked herself up from the sand and walked to the barrel. The kittens mewed happily. Jason didn't like to contradict her, but, as far as he could tell, they were enjoying the adventure.

Jason still couldn't get over the fact that Dulcinea didn't have a tail. Her hindquarters were as round as an orange; her back legs were high and stilty, giving her a stiff-legged walk which he found quite comical.

Dulcinea, turning around just then, saw Jason grinning. "You don't have to stare," she said.

"I didn't mean to," Jason apologized. "But I've never seen cats without tails. Were you born that way?"

"I most certainly was," Dulcinea said. "So was my mother, my grandmother, my great-grandmother, and so on as far back as anyone can remember. I'll have you know I come from one of the oldest families in Spain. We have been associated with the most distinguished nobility—at least nine grandees, one cardinal, three admirals . . ." Dulcinea pronounced a string of Spanish names that Jason tried hopelessly to follow.

"Not one of my kittens has a tail either, I'm proud to say." Dulcinea continued, "In my family, we have always considered a tail as not quite refined."

Gareth, who had been idly waving his own tail against the sand, suddenly pulled it around his haunches.

"Nothing personal, of course," Dulcinea added quickly. "Everyone isn't so fortunate as to be born without one."

For the sake of the kittens, Gareth suggested locating

food and fresh water. Somewhere, too, there was bound to be a village. "I'd take a chance on walking farther up the coast," he said.

Dulcinea agreed. Rather than drag the heavy barrel and to prevent the kittens from wandering off and getting lost, Jason made a knapsack of his shirt. The group set off inland, but not so far as to lose sight of the coast entirely.

Clumps of heather grew here, misty green and blue; trees leaned like flags, following the direction of the wind.

"Let's head for that big fir," Gareth said.

Dulcinea blinked questioningly. "I don't see any fur."

"*Fir!* Not *fur!* The big tree, right up there," said Gareth.

"Oh yes, of course." Dulcinea's whiskers twitched with embarrassment. "I didn't understand you."

Then, finally, as they climbed the slope, she admitted that she hadn't spent much time on land. Like her kittens, she had been born at sea.

Nevertheless, Dulcinea was the first to discover fresh water, in an ice-cold little stream that played hide-and-seek through a grove of trees. She had sniffed it out even before Gareth. From the superior expression on her face, Jason guessed that this more than made up for the misunderstanding about the fir tree.

That night, the travelers bedded down in leaves. In the morning Dulcinea was awake and up before any of them. For breakfast, she had hunted a few lizards and beetles. (Jason, who had found nothing for his own breakfast, politely declined her invitation to share the meal, although Dulcinea assured him the beetles were delicious.)

"It's amazing," Jason told Gareth, when the tailless cat was out of hearing, "how well she's managing to get along."

"Cats learned how to find their own dinners thousands of years ago," Gareth said, "and we've never forgotten."

In the course of the morning Dulcinea surprised Jason still more. On the wooded trail she moved as silently and expertly as Gareth, sometimes going even faster than he, thanks to her long hind legs. For a seagoing cat, Dulcinea had quickly learned more about the land than Jason ever expected to know. In the space of a few hours she had become as familiar with all the hidden meanings of bent twigs, broken blades of grass, the secrets of bird calls, and the direction shown by moss on a tree trunk as if she had spent her life in the forest. Not only that; Dulcinea was the first to discover humans.

"Down there," she said, "toward the coast. That's the smell of a fishing village if I ever smelled one."

This time Gareth allowed Dulcinea to lead the way. It was exactly as she had said. Just below them, hugging the shore, rose a village of thatched huts, with a small, rickety pier, boats on the sand, and nets spread for mending.

The little group headed for the nearest cottage. On the way, a tall, sunburned young man in a leather tunic almost walked into them. He paid no attention; his black brows knitted angrily, his blue eyes crackled, and he strode away without a glance behind him.

Dulcinea and the kittens hung back a little, while Jason and Gareth went to investigate the first cottage. Jason peeped through the half-open door into a small, neat room with a fire glowing on the hearth. Gareth raised his ears at a sound from the corner. In the shadows sat a dark-haired young woman, crying as if her heart would break.

15.
The Manxmen

She heard Jason's footsteps as he entered the cottage, but she did not look up. "Away with you, Baetan!" she cried. "Can you not take no for your answer? After I said I shall see no more of you?"

"I beg your pardon," Jason said. "If you said no, you probably had a good reason for it. But I'm not Baetan, and if there's anything I can do to help . . ."

The young woman wiped her face quickly with a white apron. When she raised her head, Jason saw she had one blue eye and one brown.

"You can tell that gangling, black-haired lummox to keep himself away from this cottage," she said angrily. "Else I'll have my father after him!" She began sobbing again.

Jason stood hesitantly, wondering what he could say or do; but Gareth sprang to the girl's lap, rubbed his ears against her hand, and purred so loudly that she had to stop crying and notice him. Her tears dried, and between sniffles she patted the long, black cat. Gareth rolled over and looked up at her between his paws, so solemn, and kittenish at the same time, that the girl had to laugh.

Then Jason told her about the shipwreck and the kittens, and asked if she could spare a little food and water. "We'll move on, of course," Jason added. "I was only hoping that tonight . . ."

"Move on?" she cried. "Not a bit of it! Bring in the little ones, all of them. Our old cat died two years ago and we've had none after. There's few enough cats on the island. Hurry! It's been long since I've seen a kitten."

Jason lost no time calling Dulcinea and her family. The girl knelt on the floor.

"How handsome they are!" she marveled. "How strange, without a tail. But they look all the better for it. So strong and neat." She went on, never stopping her praises, while the kittens pounced at her apron strings.

Dulcinea, keeping an eye on the little ones, sat on her haunches near the fire and looked perfectly comfortable.

"Are they yours?" the girl asked Jason. "Would you give me one?"

"They're not mine," Jason said. "But if Dulcinea likes it here, and she certainly seems to, I don't see why you can't keep them all."

The girl was so pleased at this that she hurried to the cupboard and put down seven small bowls of fish. Immediately, Dulcinea and the little ones, were eating and purring.

"Look at them," said the girl. "I know they'll be happy here. And they shall stay."

The girl's name, Jason learned, was Awin. That evening when her father, Maughold, came back from fishing, he was as delighted as his daughter with the new arrivals. Maughold was sun-blackened and gray-headed, with a broad, friendly face and a nose that jutted out like one of the cliffs of the island. He, too, played with the kittens, pretending to swat at them with his rough sailor's hands. The kittens made a game of leaping for his fingers and hanging on by their claws; but Maughold's hands, scarred by fish knives and toughened by salt water, were as hard as leather. One kitten clung to each finger while Maughold pulled them across the floor—(the sixth kitten tried to climb up his jacket).

After dinner Maughold sat back in his chair and took Dulcinea on his lap, as if she had always lived in the house. Stroking the tailless cat, he talked of his day on the boat: the catch of herring, the bad weather.

"I did not see Baetan out this day," he added.

"Baetan was here," Awin said, with a flash of annoyance. "I sent him away. For the last time, I hope."

"Ah, that would be nothing to take pride in," Maughold said, shaking his head sadly. "Why must you treat him so cruelly? The poor lad's sick for the love of you, and you cannot tell me you have nothing in your heart for him. I've seen you watch him when you thought he was not looking."

Awin turned away. "I want none of him."

"If your mother were only alive," Maughold sighed. "It is a woman's work to tell you how wrong you are."

"No," Awin said. Then, to Jason's surprise, she added, "No man wants an ugly woman. No woman wants to be married out of pity. Look at me!" she cried. "Have you not seen my eyes often enough? One blue! One brown!"

"And what is that to Baetan?" Maughold asked. "I'm sure he likes one as well as the other. He's as impartial as a herring's backbone, for he favors neither side and is attached to both!"

"I am too ugly!" Awin sobbed, and hid her face in the apron.

"Ugly?" asked Maughold. "Beauty is inside, not on the face. And the handsomest lass on the island would be ugly if she believed herself so. If a person thinks he's ugly, why then he begins to act in an ugly, cruel way. As you do now with Baetan!"

Awin heard no more, for she ran from the room and slammed the door behind her.

The name of the island was Man; the people, Manxmen. It was a tiny spot in the sea between Ireland and England. Jason wondered whether the fishermen were Irish or English.

"A little of both," Gareth said, "and neither one nor the other. As much as anything, they're Norsemen; long ago, some of their ancestors were Vikings."

Jason knew the Vikings were great sailors and could well believe the Manxmen were related to them, for they seemed more at home in their boats than anywhere else. When the men went to sea, the little village was practically deserted. Maughold, in fact, was pleased to have Jason stay and help Awin with the chores in the cottage.

The kittens showed no signs of wanting to leave. They loved the beach. Every morning they spilled out of the cottage door and raced after one another like sandpipers. They chased the gulls, who squawked indignantly at them, batted shells back and forth, and examined the tiny scuttling crabs hiding in the wet sand. Often, small waves crept up unexpectedly and washed over their paws. The tailless kittens leaped wildly then; one of them tried to chase the waves back to the sea.

When the fishermen launched their boats in the surf, the kittens were always underfoot—curious, eager to jump aboard. Those times, Dulcinea called them back with a firm commanding mew.

"As I said before," Dulcinea told Jason and Gareth, when they were alone, "I want nothing more to do with the sea. The little ones will simply have to enter another profession. No kitten of mine will sail on a boat as long as I have anything to say about it."

When news came that Sir Francis Drake and the English fleet had defeated the Armada, Jason suggested that Dulcinea might go to England, even to Queen Elizabeth's court in London.

"Yes," Dulcinea mused. "A life at court might be suitable."

Yet she made no attempt to follow Jason's suggestion, although he and Gareth offered to voyage with her. If anything, Dulcinea seemed to be making herself quite at home on the Isle of Man. She had a favorite corner near the fireplace; and she never failed to jump on Maughold's lap when he returned, smelling of salt and fog.

Jason believed that Dulcinea did not dislike the sea as much as she pretended. Some days, after calling the kittens away from the shore, Dulcinea would go down to the beach herself and watch the boats until they disappeared. Then she would sit alone by the hour, gazing out to sea.

Awin, too, sat alone. When he was ashore, Baetan would always stop by the cottage—and Awin would always make sure she was busy until he went away again. Afterwards, Awin would sit on a chair in front of the cottage and, like Dulcinea, stare across the water.

Awin's only amusement was playing with the kittens, and in this Jason and Gareth were happy to join her.

"They're funny-looking little things," Jason said, watching Awin out of the corner of his eye.

"Funny-looking?" Awin said indignantly. "I think they're beautiful."

"So do I, really," said Jason. "I just wanted to see if you'd agree with me."

Awin gave a short laugh. "What a silly thing to do. I thought they were beautiful the first moment I saw them."

"Then I can't understand it," Jason said. "They're different from ordinary cats, and yet you like them. But you still worry because your eyes are different from other people's. That doesn't make sense to me."

Awin turned away. "It's no concern of yours."

"Dulcinea is very proud because she *doesn't* have a tail," Jason went on. "She feels very distinguished about it."

"And how would a boy know what's in a cat's mind?" asked Awin.

"I . . . I can guess," Jason said. "Look at her yourself; look at the way she holds her head."

"Yes," Awin reluctantly admitted. "She is a proud cat."

"Then why shouldn't you be proud, too?" Jason asked.

Awin flushed. "Away with you, boy," she said quickly. "There's work to be done."

That night Jason noticed Awin glancing at herself in

a tiny mirror which she hid away in her apron as soon as Maughold entered the cottage. And when Baetan stopped by, her protests were not quite as strong as usual.

"Our luck's not with us," Maughold said one evening. "You'd think there wasn't a herring in the sea."

"When Dulcinea used to be a sailor's cat," Jason said, "she brought everybody luck. At least, until the shipwreck."

Maughold shook his head. "Ah, that's one cat will never go near the boats. I've watched her. She's afraid of them. So are the kittens. No, they're real house cats." He sighed heavily. "More's the pity. We could use a little luck. If things keep on this way, there'll be empty stomachs in the village."

On his lap, Dulcinea looked up questioningly at the fisherman.

Maughold stroked her head. "But there's nothing you can do about it, old girl," he said.

Before dawn Jason and Gareth woke to the sound of the fishermen shouting to each other, hauling their boats into the surf. Boy and cat went outdoors into the chilly blue mist. Dulcinea was there ahead of them, sitting on the doorstep, watching. The kittens sat solemnly next to her. Awin was there, too; and her eyes, Jason saw, were on Baetan.

At the water's edge, Maughold stopped and waved good-bye to his daughter. "And you, too, old girl," he called to Dulcinea. "Mind you're waiting for us when we come back. Wish us all luck!"

Dulcinea crouched forward, her body quivering. But she did not move from the doorstep.

Further down the beach Baetan waved at Awin. "And me?" he cried. "Awin, will you not at least wish me luck?"

Awin raised her hand timidly. "Luck, Baetan," she whispered. Then, suddenly, apron flying, she ran to the beach and into Baetan's arms.

"I guess," Jason said to Gareth, "she decided she was pretty after all."

"Everybody is," Gareth said, "if they give themselves a chance."

A gray and black streak shot past Jason's legs. It was Dulcinea, running as fast as her stilty legs would carry her, straight for Maughold. The kittens sped after her. Each one leaped into a different boat.

The little fishing fleet drove into the waves, a kitten at every bow. In Maughold's boat, Dulcinea sat proudly—a sea cat once again.

The tide foamed over the beach. The ocean filled the footprints where a boy and a cat had stood.

b.s.

Germany

•

1600

16.
The Witch Village

The waves turned into the peaked roofs of a village in Germany. The clouds hung motionless above the mountains; the sun shone brightly. But across the empty market place, the buildings were as silent as unused toys. The closed shutters turned the houses blind.

Gareth arched his neck and sniffed the air. "There's something coppery and smoky, like wood burning. Something sour and bitter that stings my nose and makes me feel crackly."

"Can you tell what it is?" Jason asked.

"Yes," Gareth said. "That's what fear smells like. I think we'd better move along." He headed for the far side of the cobbled square.

Jason hurried after him. At the corner, something buzzed past Jason's head. A stone rattled over the street. It had barely missed Gareth. Another whistled closer to the black cat.

Gareth put down his ears and ran. Behind him, Jason clattered into a winding street. Gareth ducked around a corner and skidded through a dark alleyway. By the time Jason caught up with him, the cat had sprung to one of the slanting roofs.

These, Jason realized, were the backs of the houses overlooking the square. Stone walls rose on all sides of him and shut out the sun. Gareth climbed to a chimney. Midway, he stopped, crouched, and bent his head to the roof as if inspecting a mousehole.

Jason clambered after him. "Gareth!" he whispered as loud as he could. "This is no time to look for mice!"

Gareth waved his tail. "It isn't mice," he said. "See for yourself."

Jason noticed a crack between the timbers of the roof. He put his eye to it and found he could see directly into a little chamber below.

There, wearing what looked like a nightshirt painted with strange designs, a sharp-nosed man was puttering around a three-legged brazier. He dropped a pinch of something on the glowing coals and a cloud of smoke puffed up.

"By the spirit of Zazamonkh!" the man exclaimed, picking up a long rod and tracing a circle at his feet. He went tramping around the circle, first in one direction, then the other. With his pointed nose and shaking jowls, he looked very much like a turkey.

"Asmodeus! Ahriman! Beelzebub!" the man cried. "Appear! I command you!"

The turkey-faced man stopped walking in circles. He picked up a large pot, dipped his fingers into it, and brought out a sticky gob of ointment. This he proceeded to rub over his face, head, and arms. "Spirits, I conjure you!" he shouted.

Nothing happened. The man dropped his pot of ointment and his magic rod, and sat down disgustedly in the middle of the circle.

"Why, he's a sorcerer!" said Jason. "He's trying to cast a spell."

"He isn't very good at it, either," said Gareth. "Come on."

Gareth let himself slide down the roof. Jason picked his way carefully, then jumped to the ground.

"We'll go through here," Gareth said. "It should bring us out at the end of the street. We'll be hidden most of the way. I hope whoever threw that rock isn't waiting for us. His aim might have improved."

Where the alley ended, cat and boy made a dash across the open square. Hurrying along, staying close to the walls, they soon reached the outskirts of the village. There, in a garden, an old woman was pulling up radishes. It was the first sign of life they had seen.

As soon as the woman caught sight of them, she straightened up. The radishes tumbled out of her apron.

"Hurry! Hurry!" she cried. "Get into the house!"

Before Jason knew what was happening, she seized his shoulders and pushed him to the cottage door. Gareth bounded into the room ahead of them.

"Foolish boy," the woman exclaimed. "On the streets, in broad daylight—with a cat!" Hurriedly she locked the door and slammed the shutters tight.

"But we were only walking by," Jason said.

"That's enough," she said. "I can tell you're strangers here. Haven't they come to your village yet? I thought they were everywhere."

"Who hasn't come?" Jason asked.

"The witch hunters," said the woman, "who else? It's been like this for months. Somebody—I don't even know who—started the idea that there were witches here. Since then, we've had no peace. If anyone stubs his toe or gets sick, if anyone's garden doesn't grow right—there's a witch to blame!

"The witch hunters find them," the woman went on. "That is, they'll find *somebody*. It doesn't matter who. After that, it's terrible. I can't talk about what they do to them.

"And the cats! Oh, the poor little things. They say devils hide in them. Two days ago the witch hunters drowned fifty—and burned another fifty. Poor suffering animals. My little tabby was with them."

The woman sank to a chair and shook with weeping.

Jason put his hand on her shoulder. The woman turned a tear-stained face to him. "I couldn't save mine," she sobbed. "I've tried to help the others, but it's little use.

"There's no kind of worriment or wickedness they won't put on a cat," she went on. "Cats bring on hail storms, they say, and winds. Cats have the evil eye, to bewitch whatever they look at. They can turn themselves invisible or fly through the air. They take the shape of a witch, and a witch takes the shape of a cat. It's all one and the same.

"The witch hunters catch more cats than I can ever save," she added. "Now there's hardly one left in the village. And my little tabby is gone!"

The woman began sobbing again. Gareth sprang to her lap. Rubbing his head against her cheek, purring and kneading gently with his claws, he tried all the ways known to a cat to comfort her.

She calmed a little and stroked Gareth gratefully. "You must go to the miller," she told Jason. "Master Johannes. Tell him that Mistress Ursulina begs him to help you and your cat. Master Johannes is the only man in Lindheim with all his wits in his head. He is an honest man, he knows cats are no devils. Why, he himself says the mice would destroy his grain without a cat to guard it.

"I have sent others to Master Johannes," she said. "He will treat you with kindness."

She wiped her eyes with her apron. "But I can tell you need something to eat," Mistress Ursulina said.

From a cupboard she took down bread and cheese for Jason and herself and carefully poured a bowl of milk for Gareth.

Gareth had hardly begun to lap the milk and Jason was in the midst of putting a morsel of cheese to his lips when a loud knocking rattled the cottage door.

Mistress Ursulina started up. "Out of sight!" she cried. "These days, visitors bring only trouble." Hurriedly she drew Jason to the cupboard. It was barely high enough for him to squeeze into. Gareth perched on a shelf. Mistress Ursulina hobbled to the door.

"So it's you," she said, without trying to hide her annoyance.

"I wish you a good afternoon," Jason heard an oily voice answer. "I was passing your cottage and I said to myself, ah, perhaps this is the day Mistress Ursulina will make up her mind."

"If you were passing my cottage, Master Speckfresser," said the woman, "you have come far out of your way for nothing. You are right. I have made up my mind," she went on firmly, "as I made it up long ago. The answer is no, and no again!"

"Tut, tut, tut," clucked Master Speckfresser. "You show your temper too much. What use is the field to you? My own land is on three sides of it. I should like to fill out my property, a reasonable aim for one in my position. But it is not reasonable for you to refuse to sell."

"You may be the richest man in Lindheim," Mistress Ursulina answered, "but that piece of ground belongs to me. It is my garden; I have cared for it; it is the only little happiness of my old age."

"If you will not sell," Master Speckfresser said, "I must remind you, dear lady, there are other ways to get the land I want." His voice turned cold. "The town council takes over the property of a witch—after she has been duly roasted, of course," he added. "As head of the council, I decide what happens to the property."

"You would denounce me as a witch!" cried the woman. "You dare not! I have done nothing."

"That remains to be seen," said Master Speckfresser. "If I were to say that I had seen you casting spells or riding on a broomstick, would the judges take the word of an old hag against the word of Master Speckfresser?

"I see the table is set for two," Master Speckfresser continued. "Yet there is only one of you. And . . . ," he paused a moment, "something else. When did a cupboard start wearing shoes?"

He strode across and flung open the door. "A boy! And a cat! Better and better! Are these your familiars? Does this black cat do your devil's work?"

Gareth spat and bushed his tail.

"Aha!" cried Speckfresser. "The devil fears the powers of righteousness!"

"He doesn't fear you!" Jason shouted angrily. "He doesn't fear anything! I heard what you said. If you try to hurt Mistress Ursulina, I'll tell them all about it!"

Master Speckfresser's face turned purple and his cheeks trembled. He shook his fist at Jason. "Threaten me?" he sputtered. "I think the council will be interested to know Mistress Ursulina has been entertaining demons!"

Master Speckfresser turned on his heel and stamped out of the cottage.

Mistress Ursulina clapped a hand to her forehead. "You have ruined yourself, poor boy. Now they will arrest you, too!"

"But if I tell them what happened," Jason insisted, "how can they harm any of us? We aren't witches, and my cat isn't a devil, and that's all there is to that."

"Son, son," Mistress Ursulina cried, "don't you understand? That makes no difference. Once they accuse, there is no hope. You must go to Master Johannes at once. He will hide you; he will help you get out of the village."

"I'm not going to run away," Jason said.

"You must!"

"Then you come with us," said Jason. "If you don't, we'll stay right here."

"Very well," Mistress Ursulina sighed. "But you shall go on ahead. The three of us must not be seen together. That will fit Master Speckfresser's plan too well."

From a corner she took a wicker basket. "Here, carry your cat in this." She put the basket on the floor.

Jason quickly put Gareth inside and closed the lid. "I'll

tell Master Johannes you're on your way to the mill," he said.

"Yes, yes," said the woman. "But hurry!"

Limping along as fast as she could, she led Jason out of the cottage.

"Go past the fields," Mistress Ursulina directed. "Then turn left. The mill is there, by the stream."

Clutching the basket, Jason set off along the road. If the days in Egypt had been the greatest times for a cat, Jason thought, the days in this village must be the worst.

But how, Jason wondered, did Master Speckfresser dare accuse the poor woman of being a witch? Jason had quickly recognized the man's sharp nose and shaking jowls. It was Master Speckfresser who had been wearing the painted nightshirt, with grease smeared all over his head.

17.
Speckfresser Calls Two Demons

Master Johannes was the biggest man Jason had ever seen. He was at work in his low stone house, whistling merrily between his teeth and covered with flour from head to foot. While the mill wheel clattered noisily in the stream outside, Johannes carried the enormous bags of grain, one under each arm, as if they weighed no more than feather pillows. Beneath the dusting of flour, his face was ruddy and his eyes good-natured, but when Jason told him what had happened in Mistress Ursulina's cottage, the miller frowned and stopped whistling.

"Speckfresser!" he snorted. "That greedy gobbler! Well, he has Johannes to deal with now!"

Jason lifted the basket lid so Gareth could come out and stretch.

"So ho!" the miller cried. "Is this another of Speckfresser's devils?" He picked up the cat and balanced him on his outstretched palms. The miller's hands were so broad that Gareth seemed lost in them and as tiny as a kitten. "He's a handsome one," said Johannes. He set Gareth down.

Jason noticed that for all their size the miller's fingers were deft and gentle; when Johannes patted Gareth, his hands were as light as moths' wings and left behind them the same dusty traces.

Johannes took the boy and cat into the cool twilight of the mill, and made them comfortable at a sturdy wooden table.

"I've heard enough of witches," Master Johannes said. "The whole village has gone mad with them. An honest man puts his nose out the door after dark and some rogue calls him a witch! Now they have laws against witches, but the more laws they have, the more witches they find! Today, there's one in every corner. Senseless, stupid fools! Have they nothing better to think of? Let them trifle with me and my friends. They'll find Johannes a bigger handful than some poor scarecrow terrified out of his wits!"

Jason had expected Mistress Ursulina to reach the mill long before now. As the time passed, Johannes, too, began to grow anxious.

"I'll go to the cottage and find what's amiss," he said. "Wait for me. Don't stir from here."

It was well after nightfall when Master Johannes returned. The miller's face was flushed with anger.

"They've arrested her," he said grimly. "Nobody wants to talk much, but from what little I could find out, she must have changed her mind about coming here. She went to the village instead. My guess is that she told Master Speckfresser she'd sell her field. It must have been the only way she thought he would let you alone.

"Speckfresser's a gobbler, but he knows very well what

he's doing," Johannes continued. "All he had to do was accuse her of witchcraft; he'd be bound to get the land for nothing. So why should he pay? Mistress Ursulina's in prison right now, waiting to be tried. And I doubt they'll take long about it."

Jason caught his breath. A woman, a stranger, was willing to give up her life for him and Gareth. "But it's not fair," he cried. "How can Speckfresser accuse anybody? He's a sorcerer himself!"

"What's that you say?" Johannes straightened up.

Jason told the miller what he had seen on his way through the village.

"That fraud!" shouted the miller. "That cheating gobbler! I'd like to have him under my mill wheel!"

Johannes thought for a moment. "There must be something we can do. It's no good accusing *him;* it would be his word against ours. Besides, I wouldn't accuse anybody of witchcraft, not even Speckfresser, not after what I've seen them do to witches."

"Could we make him take back what he said about Mistress Ursulina?" asked Jason.

"Withdraw his charges? Not Speckfresser. Wait a minute!" The miller snapped his fingers. "There is a way. We'll have to take a chance. But if it works . . ."

The miller flung open a clothespress. Moments later, Jason was dressed all in black, with a broad black hat pulled down over his ears. With a handful of soot from the fireplace, the miller blackened Jason's face.

"Your cat's all right as he is," Johannes laughed. "Come on, now. I'll tell you my plan on the way."

In the light of a torch the miller hitched up his cart;

161

Gareth and Jason climbed on. Master Johannes slapped the reins on the horse's back and they moved off at a good trot toward the village.

Leaving Johannes at the town square, Jason followed Gareth silently to the alleyway. The cat found the back of Speckfresser's house and the two friends climbed stealthily to the roof. Gareth's eyes blazed in the moonlight.

"You look wonderful," Jason said. "Just right. Now if we're lucky . . ." He bent his head to the crack.

As Johannes had said, all depended on whether Speckfresser was trying to work his sorcery. Since the town clock had just begun tolling midnight, the witching hour, there was a good chance that he was. Still, it was no more than a chance. Jason squinted, trying to focus on the room below.

"He's there!" Jason saw the turkey-faced man, dressed as he had been the first time they had seen him tramping around his circle. "He's trying out his spells again."

"He'll never learn," murmured Gareth. "All right. I'll go first."

Gareth leaped to the chimney. He balanced on the peaked roof, over the open stone well, then dived. Jason lowered himself in after the cat. An instant later he was falling downward in a shower of soot and loose stones. His toes scraped brick and clouds of dust billowed in his face. Gareth, bristling and spitting, had already leaped from the fireplace into the chamber.

Through the drifting soot Jason saw Speckfresser, mouth open with terror, too horrified to scream. He pointed his forefinger and little finger at the cat and boy.

"You called us, master," Jason said.

Speckfresser gulped. "Called you?" he choked.

"It is your practice to summon demons," Jason went on in a hollow voice. "We are here. What is your command?"

"Now that you're here," Speckfresser said through chattering teeth, "I can't seem to think of anything. My command is: leave immediately. Both of you. Please, I didn't mean to disturb you."

Gareth, meantime, had perched on a stack of the would-be sorcerer's books of magic, where he snarled and bared his teeth in a most frightful way.

"And if you don't mind," Speckfresser pleaded, "take the smaller devil, too."

"You have disturbed others in this village," Jason said. "You have caused an old woman to be thrown into prison. You must withdraw your accusation. Otherwise, she may be burned."

"Yes, yes." Speckfresser nodded hastily. His jowls quivered. "I will withdraw . . ." He hesitated a moment. "Wait . . . why should a demon plead to save a victim from the fire? Demons delight in fires. . . ." He looked closer at Jason, then seized him by the collar.

"Demons!" he shouted. "You're no more demon than I! You're the boy in Ursulina's cupboard. That's no devil; that's only a cat!"

"Master Speckfresser," Jason said, "your game is ruined. You accused Mistress Ursulina of entertaining devils. Now you admit we aren't devils. And if we aren't, Mistress Ursulina must go free!"

"I admit nothing!" stormed Speckfresser.

"Then I'll go to the council. I'll tell them about your

spells—that don't even work. Johannes doesn't want you hurt, but this is your last chance."

"You'll never leave this room!" cried Speckfresser, snatching a sickle-shaped knife.

Jason dodged the sweeping blade. Johannes should have been here by now. The miller, too big for the chimney, had planned to burst into Speckfresser's chamber and apply some additional arguments. Jason leaped from one side to the other, as the knife whistled around his ears. Where, he thought desperately, was Johannes?

Now! With a gasp of relief, Jason heard the door splinter and crash from its hinges. Master Speckfresser had stopped in his tracks. Jason pulled the hat off and raised his head. Johannes stood in the doorway. But he was surrounded by guards.

One of the guards stepped forward and leveled his pike. "You are under arrest, all of you!"

Speckfresser threw back his head and cackled gleefully. "Try to ruin my plan? It's the bonfire for you, my lad!"

"All of you," the guard repeated gruffly. "You, too, Master Speckfresser. You ordered the arrest of Master Johannes. We caught him in the village. Then we came to you to ask for further instructions. But from what I see here . . ." the guard gestured with his pike, ". . . you're as much a witch as anyone. That means automatic arrest."

"I'm not a witch!" Speckfresser shrieked. He dropped to his knees. "My spells don't work. Ask the boy, ask the cat. It was only amusement," he babbled. "Let Ursulina go free. I can explain. . . ."

"You'll have a chance to do that," said the guard, "when you meet the judges. Now move!"

18.
The Verdict

Four humans and one cat huddled on the damp straw of the cell. It was too dark to see Master Speckfresser's face, but Jason imagined it wouldn't be very jolly.

"Leave off that sniveling and whining, you gobbler," Master Johannes ordered impatiently. "It's your fault we're all here. If you hadn't lied and tried to swindle honest people . . ."

Master Speckfresser sniffed again. "I'm sorry," he said in a tiny voice. "I never thought it would turn out this way."

"I'm quite sure you didn't," said Jason.

"It's hard to believe things can be so disagreeable," the wretched Speckfresser snuffled, "until they happen to you."

Mistress Ursulina quietly stroked Gareth.

Johannes shifted uncomfortably on the hard stone floor. "What I don't understand," the big miller said, "is why you kept on with that ridiculous sorcery business. You should have seen it didn't work. And if it had, I'm sure you wouldn't have liked the results."

"After all the talk in the village about witches," Speckfresser said "—how they fly through the air, make themselves invisible, turn straw into gold—I just thought to myself, why not try it. I always wanted to do those things."

"Well, they can't be done," said the miller. "And if you'd put as much effort into honest work as you did into those spells, you'd have had all the gold you wanted."

"Yes, you're right," Speckfresser sighed. A large tear rolled down his nose. "But I'll explain everything. The judges will listen to me."

A few hours later, however, when the guards led Jason and the others to the council room, the judges hardly glanced at Master Speckfresser. The eldest judge, a bony, black-robed man with a lantern jaw and eyes as sharp as thorns, shuffled through some parchment sheets on the table. "We have studied your cases thoroughly," he began, licking his lips, as if tasting every word.

"You've had no time to study anything," shouted the miller.

The judge paid no attention. His little eyes turned sharper than ever as he read from his parchments.

"The accused witch, Johannes the miller: guilty.

"The accused witch, Ursulina: guilty.

"The accused witch, Master Speckfresser: guilty.

"One demon disguised as a boy disguised as a demon: guilty.

"One demon disguised as a cat: guilty."

The judge set down his papers. "You will be burned at the stake in the morning. Believe me," he added with a smile, "this is all for your own good."

"We'll decide our own good!" Johannes jumped up. With one motion of his powerful arms, he tipped over the judge's table. The sheets of parchment went flying. The guards, who had been half-dozing, sprang forward. In the confusion one dropped his pike and stumbled into his neighbor. Seizing a chair in one hand, the burly miller laid about him. A window smashed. One of the miller's fists sent a guard sprawling to the wall.

"Out, friends!" bellowed Johannes. "This is no place for an honest man!"

The judges shouted at the guards; the guards shouted at each other. "The demons are loose! Warn the village!"

The miller battered his way through the door, then snatched Ursulina and put her over his shoulder. Jason and Gareth tumbled down the steps into the market place, with Speckfresser, gasping and gurgling, bring up the rear.

The miller's cart was still tied near the alleyway behind Speckfresser's house. The band of escaping demons leaped onto it. The alarm bell in the stone tower began ringing frantically. The frightened horses dashed forward and the cart lurched after them.

The road through the forest stretched quietly ahead in the moonlight. With the village far behind, Johannes dropped the reins and let his horses set their own pace.

"They won't come after us now," Johannes said, while the cartwheels creaked over scattered leaves. "They really think we're demons—that's the ridiculous part of it. And I doubt they have the stomach for chasing demons after dark."

"I owe you my life, Master Johannes," said Ursulina. "But you have lost your mill, your trade . . ."

"A miller can always find a mill waiting for him," Johannes laughed. "And you shall keep house for me."

"What about me?" Master Speckfresser piped up.

"Oh, you. Well, if you behave yourself, Speckfresser, you can be my apprentice. I'll teach you how to work for a change."

"Me, a miller?" Speckfresser clucked. "Why . . ." When he saw the look Master Johannes gave him, he stopped. ". . . naturally. It should be a very healthy life. I always enjoy bread."

When the cart reached a turn in the road Gareth seemed to grow restless. "I think we'd better leave you here," Jason told the miller.

Johannes, Ursulina, and even Master Speckfresser protested. But there was a tone in Jason's voice which the miller could not deny. He reined up the cart and clapped Jason on the shoulder.

"Good luck, boy. If you should change your mind, you can still catch up with us on this road."

Jason and Gareth hopped down, and the cart pulled away.

"I'll be glad to get out of here," Jason said. "This is a terrible place. It's bad enough for humans, but what about the cats? If these people keep on there won't be any cats left!"

"They'll stop someday," Gareth said. "For a while. Then they'll start up again, a little differently, but still much the same. And so it will go, off and on, until people stop being superstitious, afraid of the dark and afraid of each other."

"But in the meantime, what can you do?"

"Survive," said Gareth. "And hope."

Jason shook his head. "In Egypt they thought you were a god. Here they think you're a demon. Won't anyone ever understand you're a cat?"

"We're waiting," said Gareth. "It takes patience. But that's one thing cats have a lot of. Why, even a kitten knows if you wait long enough someone's bound to open the door."

Jason could still see the cart in the distance. In the moonlight he glimpsed Master Johannes raising his hand. Jason raised his own hand in farewell. The cart lumbered out of sight.

Then the road was completely empty.

America

•

1775

19.
Parker'f Perpetual Moufetrapf

There was still a road, but it had changed. Under a sky streaked with the pale blue of early spring the fields whispered like sleepers about to waken. Jason pulled the flaps of his three-cornered hat over his ears and turned up his jacket collar. Gareth padded ahead, his eyes narrowed against the breeze.

Behind him Jason heard the clop-clop of hoofs, and turned to see a gaily painted wagon swing around a bend of the road. A sheet of canvas rose like a tent over the front half of the wagon. Boxes, bolts of cloth, teakettles, pots, and pans filled the back.

The driver, a lanky lean fellow, with eyes as bright as a bird's, wore an enormous cocked hat with a bunch of rooster feathers pinned to it. As soon as he saw Jason he gave a warbling, triple-toned whistle. The horse moved a bit faster, and soon the wagon was abreast of Jason and Gareth.

"You won't get far at the rate you're going," the driver called. "Hop in, you and your furry companion. You can ride to Boston if you aren't in a hurry."

Gareth jumped to the wooden seat. Jason hoisted himself up after the cat.

The driver raised his hat. "Gentlemen," he said, addressing Gareth as well as Jason, "allow me to present myself. Professor Peter Perseverance Parker at your service, holder of ninety-seven different honors, orders, medals, and the highest recommendations from the crowned heads of every continent. At present engaged in the enlightenment and instruction of his fellow countrymen."

"Does that mean you're a teacher?" Jason asked.

"In the very noblest sense of the word, my boy," said Professor Parker, reaching over and pulling a coin from Jason's ear. "Instruction can take many forms. My unwavering goal is to bring the benefits of civilization to the honest toilers in the farthest reaches of this terrestrial paradise. Instruction, in that case, may take the form of a humble pot or pan."

"Oh, you're a peddler." Jason nodded.

"A peddler?" Professor Parker drew himself up indignantly. "How can you term an undertaking of such magnitude mere peddling?" He bent and pulled a coin from Gareth's ear. "Consider this shilling—in itself no more than a piece of metal. But when it buys a teakettle, a packet of pins, a yard of cloth—it is gloriously translated into comfort and convenience. It is my solemn duty to help in that translation. Of course, I do have my own specialties." He drew a handbill from his sleeve and passed it over to Jason who studied it with interest.

At first Jason couldn't quite make it out, until he realized all the S's had been printed as long, sloping F's:

PERPETUAL MOUʃETRAPʃ!!!

Profeſſor Parker offerſ, at a Modeſt
Priſe, to thoſe in Neede of Them,
Nature'ſ fineſt Mouſetrap. If well
car'd for and given much Loving Kindneſſ,
they will be

    GUARANTEED TO PLEAſE!!!

"Mousetraps?" Jason asked.

"Nature's finest, as my advertisement states," said the Professor. "Look in the back of the wagon."

Jason turned around, lifted a flap of the tent, and peered down at a dozen neat wicker cages, each one holding a chubby kitten.

"Those kittens," the Professor said, "have been given to me by some of the finest families in Boston, who ask only a good home for them. It is my task to see that they get it. Ask anyone in the colonies."

Jason relaxed a little. Although he seriously doubted that Professor Parker had ninety-seven medals, Jason somehow had the feeling that he really did like cats. Besides, Gareth always seemed to know whom he could trust, and the black cat was resting calmly on the seat.

"What civilization would be complete without a cat?" the Professor went on. "What greater blessing to the home than the kindly yet watchful eye of this tiger of the fireside? Parker's Perpetual Mousetraps are known far and wide. Why, without my services I doubt if you'd find a cat west of Boston."

By this time the wagon was rattling into a little village. As soon as the children spied it, they left their games to race after it. The Professor reined up near the village green and the children clustered around him. The Professor whistled some fancy bird calls, pulled coins out of ears, and even juggled three flashing balls. The village women hurried to look at the stocks of cloth and tinware. The spare, weathered men, some carrying muskets, examined the axes and saws.

Two men walked to the side of the wagon, where Professor Parker was displaying one of his Perpetual Mousetrap*f* to a wide-eyed little girl.

"How goes it in Boston?" Jason heard one of them ask.

Professor Parker put down the wicker cage. Jason expected the Professor to begin one of his speeches about a glorious something or other. Instead, his face turned grim and he spoke very quietly.

"A keg of powder," he said, "waiting for the spark."

"We'll be ready if we're called," the man said.

"You'll have the news as soon as it comes," Professor Parker answered. "Sam Adams has horsemen to carry it. Do you drill your men?"

"Every day. Give us a minute's notice and there'll be fifty of us to go against the Lobsterbacks. But we need more muskets, more powder and shot."

"So do we all," Professor Parker said. "Hancock's doing everything he can. We're gathering our supplies. Don't think it's easy in Boston. Adams and Hancock don't dare show their faces. There's an order for their arrest."

The man whistled through his teeth. "The Lobsters have gone that far then?"

"They'll go farther," Professor Parker said. "They'll push us to the wall with bayonets."

"What," cried the man angrily. "Do they take us for cowards? Let it begin now, I say. Enough is enough. I've had my fill of lobster!"

"In time, in time. You'll have your chance soon enough. Until then, keep your musket clean."

With a wink Professor Parker took a shilling out of the man's nose and swung up on the wagon.

The wagon creaked out of the village and down the road, heading for distant farms. The horse seemed to have his own ideas about how fast to go and which way to take. Professor Parker leaned back in the seat, let the reins go slack, and tipped his feather-trimmed hat over his eyes.

"What did that man mean back there," Jason asked, "when he said he had his fill of lobster?"

"*Homarus vulgaris,* the European lobster, as opposed to *Homarus americanus,* the tasty denizen of our American waters. The British variety of *Homarus vulgaris* also abounds in these parts and is notable for its bright red coat and large claws, which snap at everything within reach. A very prickly customer, especially when carrying a musket with bayonet. In short, my boy, a Lobster, a Lobsterback, a Redcoat—whatever you choose to call it. I call it a plague, visited upon us by His Most Gracious and Incredibly High Stubbornness, King George the Third.

"Our friend in the village," Professor Parker went on, "did not mean to imply that he had his fill of *Homarus americanus*. Of the other variety, I dare say we have all had our fill. We have paid our taxes to the mighty King of Lobsters, and taxes on the taxes; we have asked this crabby Lobster King to treat us as men, to give us the same rights as any of his other subjects, to give us what belongs to us in the first place. Since he refuses . . . ," Professor Parker shrugged, "what can we do but take them?"

Jason looked silently at the Professor for a long moment. "First I thought you were a teacher," he said. "Then I thought you were a peddler. Now I don't think you're either one."

Professor Parker chuckled. "Why not a little of both? A peddler can carry some ideas along with his pots and pans. Liberty's a big idea," said the Professor. "But it can fit in a teakettle. I sell the teakettles, and put in the liberty free of charge."

"But what about the kittens?" Jason asked.

"I'll have to get busy about that," Professor Parker said. "There's a lot of Perpetual Mousetraps waiting for homes. You know," he added, "countries are like cats. They like to settle down in their own ways. But they want their freedom, too. They'll fight for it if they have to."

"I know my cat won't let anybody order him around," Jason said, giving Gareth an admiring pat.

"Especially not lobsters," added the Professor. "Well, that's the way it is here. And if things keep on, there's going to be the biggest cat and lobster fight you ever saw!"

20.
The Return

That night they camped along the road. At dawn Professor Parker hitched up the horse, slapped the reins, and after a few miles turned in at a farmhouse. Here, the farmer was tall, black-bearded, with heavy callouses on his hands. Jason talked with him and learned that he and his family had come from Canada, and, before that, from France, but he called himself an American now. He had not owned the farm long, and after the last harvest the rats had almost ruined his grain.

Professor Parker sold him two kittens. "They will grow up with the land," he told the farmer, "and they will love it as much as you do. They will work as hard as you do, not because they are slaves but because they are creatures of freedom, living their lives as is natural for them."

At the next farm Jason met a little girl as pretty and happy as the April morning. She clapped her hands with delight when the Professor's wagon appeared; but, unlike the other children, she did not run to greet him. Jason saw why. The little girl was lame.

To her, Professor Parker offered one of the finest and most beautiful of all the kittens.

"He will race and leap and climb trees for her," he told Jason later. "And, because he will love her, it will be just as if she herself were doing all those things. She will see his courage and it will remind her to keep up her own. If she should ever cry—and all of us do, sometime or another— he will have velvet paws to comfort her."

Farther down the road Professor Parker drove up to a small cottage. Here lived an elderly couple, whose children and grandchildren had grown up and who were happy to spend their days looking after their own plot of ground.

When they learned that Professor Parker had kittens in the wagon, they were as pleased as if the little cats had been their own young grandchildren. They chose a handsome black-and-white kitten with green eyes.

"In the evenings," Professor Parker said to Jason, "when they sit by the fire and their hands touch, as they did long ago, their cat will purr quietly to them. Because a cat has many memories himself, he will understand theirs. Like them, he will be content to rest at the end of the day."

At the next farm Jason tried quickly to hide his surprise, for one of the girls of the family had the same long hair, the same laughing blue eyes as Diahan in Erin.

But her name, she told Jason, was Eileen O'Day. She put her hands on her hips and looked at him boldly. "And you've no need to stare as if you'd seen a ghost!" She turned away, but Jason noticed she glanced at him when she didn't think he'd notice.

The cat she chose was ginger-colored, the wildest of all.

"Those two will find their own mischief together," said

the Professor. "There'll be games of hide-and-seek, as well as chasing pretty ribbons. There might even be a few broken dishes; and pouting that can turn into laughter like quicksilver, and laughter that turns into tears and back again. Later, she'll whisper her dreams and secrets to him, and he will listen very solemnly. And because a cat is wise and understands secrets, he'll never breathe a word of them to anyone.

"Yes, they'll have secrets together." Professor Parker nodded. "Perhaps she'll tell him about a young lad who's caught her heart. She'll tell her cat about it before she ever tells the lad, you can be sure.

"Why, look at that," the Professor said, pretending to speak to Gareth. "I'd say the boy was blushing." Then, to show he was joking, he took a shilling out of Jason's ear.

And so it went with all the others Jason, Gareth, and Professor Parker visited. Old and young, men and women, boys and girls—each found a kitten exactly to his liking. In what seemed no time at all every kitten had found a home, and Professor Parker turned once again toward Boston.

Near the outskirts of the town a band of farmers blocked the road. Some had muskets on their shoulders; other carried pitchforks, axes, or wooden poles.

Professor Parker leaned down from the wagon. "Going on a picnic?" he called to one of the farmers.

The man gave a cold laugh. "Fishing for lobsters," he shouted back. "It started at Lexington this morning. The Redcoats are out in force now. The fat's in the fire."

Gareth pricked up his ears. In another moment Jason, too, heard the shrilling of fifes and the crisp chatter of drums coming across a field of stubble. Burning scarlet in the April sun, a column of British infantry swung around the bend of the road. There were distant shouts of command. The column turned and cut across the field like the reddened blade of a knife. At the sight of the Regulars a shout went up from the farmers. They moved forward, slowly, steadily. Professor Parker clicked his tongue at the horse. The wagon creaked ahead.

The British line advanced. To Jason, the redcoated soldiers in their high bearskin helmets looked like so many toys escaped from their box. At closer range, though, he saw the sun glint blindingly on their muskets and sharp bayonets. His heart beat rapidly in his throat and he could not swallow. Instinctively, Jason picked up Gareth and held the black cat in his arms.

The fifes shrieked in his ears. Like a thousand mocking whistles, the sound was even more frightening than the sight of the Regulars. The British had halted and now stood motionless, but the fifing never stopped. Another command rang out above the noise. Jason saw the Regulars level their rifles. The farmers hesitated, then moved forward.

The sword of a British officer flashed downward; the snick of flintlocks rattled along the scarlet line. Jason saw the flash and then heard the musketry crack like a giant whip. The Minutemen raced through the drifting smoke toward the Regulars, firing, reloading, crouching behind hillocks and large clumps of grass.

"By the Great King of Lobsters!" Professor Parker shouted, "we're attacking a British line!"

The lurch of the wagon threw Jason and Gareth forward. There was a second volley of musket fire. Jason heard a man cry out and saw another slump to the ground.

"Stay in the wagon!" the Professor shouted. "I'm going

to unhitch the horse. We've got to let the Sons of Liberty know, back there . . ." He jerked his head in the direction of the road they had traveled.

The Professor worked furiously at the harness. Another volley came from the Regulars. Professor Parker staggered against the wagon. Jason leaped down. The Professor was pressing his hands against his chest. His face had gone gray.

"*Homarus vulgaris* is a prickly customer, I told you that." He grinned. "Listen, boy. Can you ride back that far and that fast? Give the horse his head. He knows the way."

"But you can't . . . ," Jason began.

"Get out of here, boy," Professor Parker said. "I'll stay here and see they don't put grapeshot into my teakettles." He smiled and tried to pull a shilling out of Jason's ear, but his hand went slack and the coin dropped to the earth.

The Regulars had brought a fieldpiece into action. Canister shot tore at the fence and the budding branches.

The horse reared as Jason and Gareth climbed on its back. Bending forward, Jason flung his arms around the animal's neck; Gareth clung to its mane.

It was nightfall, after nightfall, after midnight. . . . Jason had no idea of the time when the lathered horse finally pounded into the village where the Professor had first stopped. Lantern light shone in his face. The men crowded around him. He could answer none of their questions. Whether the attack had been successful, whether the Regulars had broken, whether the battle continued, he did not know. He knew only that Professor Parker had told him to deliver word that the fighting had begun. This much he had done.

Torches flamed throughout the village. The farmers were harnessing their horses, hitching up wagons.

Jason, his clothes stiff and stained, tried to make his way through the crowd. "Let me ride back with somebody," he pleaded. "The Professor's there. . . ." His words were lost in the shouts of the men, the stamping and whickering of the horses. Then the village green was empty.

Jason sat down on a stone. "They wouldn't take me," he said bitterly.

Gareth, nearly white from the dust of the road, rubbed against Jason's legs.

Jason raised his head. "I'll go after them."

"No," Gareth said, "this is their battle. They'll fight it for you—this time, at least."

The cat walked a few paces from the green, stopped, and looked back at Jason. "Come," he said. "Follow me."

Darkness. Not quite darkness. To Jason, it felt as though he were climbing a gently sloping hill. He could make out Gareth beside him, striding forward, his neck out, head alert, and tail straight behind him—the way Gareth always walked when he had something serious on his mind.

Half-light. Half-shadow. Jason could not be sure whether these were the hills of Erin or Germany. Perhaps they were the forests of Britain. It was hard to say. The trees kept changing and shifting before his eyes. For the first time he was deeply frightened. He had been frightened before, but this was different. This was a trembling, questioning thing, like the wing of a fledgling bird. Suddenly, he feared he would lose sight of Gareth in the shadows. He bent and took the cat in his arms.

"Where are we going?" Jason asked.

"We're going home," Gareth said.

Home! Jason had rarely thought of it; they had been so busy. It was as if all the times Jason *hadn't* thought about home all gathered together and turned into wanting to go home. Yes, yes, he thought to himself, like a flame leaping up. But underneath it was a curious kind of sadness.

"I do want to go home," Jason said, "but do we have to do it right now? Can't we . . ."

"No," Gareth said, in a voice that allowed no further questions. "I'm sorry. It must be now. Don't forget, I took you with me this time because it was a special occasion."

"It certainly was," Jason said appreciatively.

"More than you might imagine," said Gareth. "You see, there's a certain moment that comes—even for a kitten —when you have to start thinking about growing up. That's a very special occasion. It begins by learning new things."

"I learned a lot about cats . . . and different places," Jason said.

"That was only part of it," said Gareth. "If you think back, everybody we met had something to tell you—about themselves, and about yourself. It's a way of finding out a part of what you have to know to be a grown-up."

"You mean," Jason began, "when you took me along you were sort of letting me practice, the way you did in Japan with the kittens?"

"You might say that," Gareth agreed.

"I think I understand," Jason said, after a moment. "But I'll still miss them all. Cerdic Longtooth, Leonardo, even Speckfresser. And Diahan."

"You'll find them again," Gareth reassured him. "Not

exactly the way you remember them now. But you'll find them, you can be sure of it."

"Maybe so," Jason said glumly. "But I'll never be allowed to make another trip like this after we get home."

"You'll make other trips," Gareth said. "The journey isn't over. If you want to know the truth, it's really just starting. You'll make you own voyages even farther."

"Well," said Jason, a little more cheerfully, "I guess I'd like that. It would be just as much fun, wouldn't it? And think of all the things we'd have to talk about."

"Yes, that's true," Gareth said slowly. "But I won't be able to speak to you after we get back."

"Oh, no!" Jason cried. "That isn't fair! No, if that's the way it is, I don't want to go home."

"Wait now," Gareth said. "I won't be able to speak to you. That doesn't mean we won't understand each other. Don't you know by this time that cats don't need words? If you watch, and try to understand, all cats can talk."

"It won't be the same," Jason said.

"Yes it will," Gareth said. "You can say some of the loveliest things in the world—without words."

Shadows clung to them. As closely as Jason held him, the cat still faded from his arms.

"Gareth!" Jason called. "Gareth . . ."

Jason raised his head from his pillow. The black cat, stretched full length beside him, looked up and yawned. Jason rubbed his eyes. His bedroom was just as it had always been. Sunlight poured through the window. How long had he slept? It couldn't have been more than a few minutes, an hour at the most. It was still afternoon.

"Gareth?" Jason said questioningly.

The cat began a deep purr of pleasure. His claws moved in and out and he blinked at Jason.

What a dream it had been, Jason thought to himself. He frowned. Yet he remembered it so clearly. There had been Egyptians and sorcerers, Roman legionaries. Even now, wide awake, he could see the faces of each one.

"And *you* were in it, too," he said to Gareth, rubbing the black cat's ears. "You were the one who arranged the whole thing. And you know, I still think you could really do it—if you wanted to."

Jason sat up on the bed, feeling a little disappointed, wishing the dream had been real after all.

Below, he heard his mother stirring about the kitchen. He stood up and walked to the door. He remembered, suddenly, that he had been told to stay in his room. Grumbling, Jason turned and thrust his hands in his pockets. His fingers touched metal, smooth and worn. Surprised, he pulled it out. It was in the shape of a T with a loop on the crossbar.

"That's funny. I didn't have this before," Jason said. "I wonder . . ." He sat down beside Gareth. "What do you think?"

Gareth put his head to one side and looked inquiringly at Jason.

"You want me to decide for myself, is that it?" Jason asked. "Well, I think . . ."

Jason's mother was calling.

"Come on, Gareth," Jason said. "They're waiting for us." He smiled at the cat and slipped the bit of metal back into his pocket.

Then he and Gareth ran downstairs to supper.

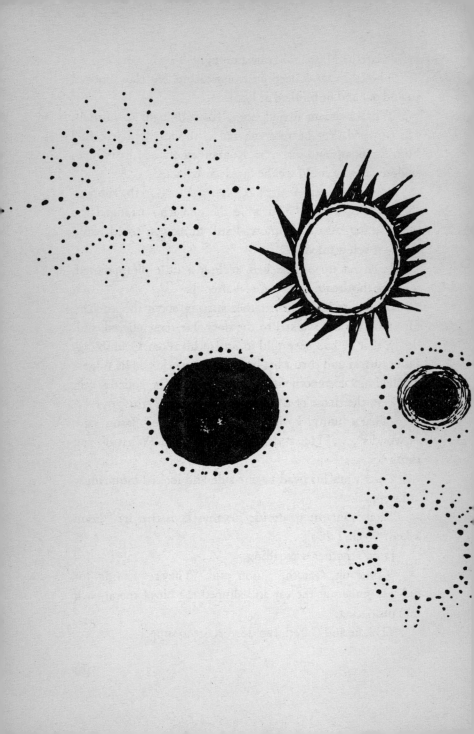